I0607648

Hell Hath No Fury

FURY

ANGELA ADDAMS

Fury
ISBN # 978-1-80250-597-9
©Copyright Angela Addams 2024
Cover Art by Kelly Martin ©Copyright March 2024
Interior text design by Claire Siemaszkiewicz
Totally Bound Publishing

Published in 2024 by Totally Bound Publishing, United Kingdom.

Totally Bound Publishing is an imprint of Totally Entwined Group Limited.

FURY

Dedication

To tenacity and the ability to withstand the storm.

Chapter One

How did the werewolf find herself in a gilded cage?
She put herself there.

Charlie

Three a.m. was the witching hour for werewolves. The darkest moments of the day, when predators prowled and prey scurried.

I had no business being out here, stalking like the land belonged to my wolf. But the moon had called to me, loudly, relentless, and I'd been restless, unable to sleep through the nightmares from my past that haunted me — the truths of what my werebeast had cost me.

Again and again.

Her presence in my life had led to murder. It had led to misunderstandings so grave that wolves under my leadership had died.

For me. *Because* of me.

It had led to my latest mistake, trying to invade the minds of the Duke clan wolves.

Bad judgment was becoming a part of who I was, apparently. That…and following instincts that took me down the wrong path.

"You're a bad girl, Charlotte." Kane's voice ricocheted through my mind. *"Careless with your actions."*

I shook off the shame, literally, tossing my fur from nape to tail. My wolf had no time for dwelling on Kane's words. That was the past. No matter how recent, she didn't care. She wanted to hunt, to lose ourselves in the smell of grass and bark, dirt, wild furry bunnies and long-legged deer.

I'd melded with her a long time ago, unlike my werebeast — the other side of me who ruled my anger — so I didn't fear losing myself in her predatory thoughts. I welcomed the distraction.

Movement to my left, a rustling of leaves, not the wind, had me turning on instinct. I lifted my nose in the direction of the sound, narrowed my eyes, piercing through the darkness. There, just in the shadows, was a warm-blooded snack.

I sculked, moving slowly, my belly close to the ground, careful not to snap twigs or disturb leaves. The doe's long legs trembled as if sensing my approach. I raised my gaze, scanning the slick body, all the way up along its neck to those big, bulbous eyes. It twitched its ears, swiveling in my direction. I was fight. She was flight. One wrong twitch and she'd be gone. I moved stealthily, my breath held, my paw pads barely making a sound. I could be a shadow, silent and looming.

A heartbeat later, the doe bolted, startled by some unknown thing. Didn't matter… Joy surged and hunger coursed through me, propelling me as I shoved off my hind legs and gave chase.

The doe crashed through thickets and leapt over fallen logs, zigzagging her way through the forest. I got close enough to nip at her hind, my canines barely scratching her skin. I raced to the side, the temptation of blood, of ripping hot meat from her throat, filled me with power. I leapt, ready to take her down, snap her neck and have my meal, soaring toward her, teeth bared, claws ready...and I missed.

The doe swerved left, and I flew right past her, landing in a heap against the thick trunk of a nearby tree. I lay panting, heaving giant breaths of disappointment. It felt good to run, to chase, to get so close. It didn't feel good to lose my reward.

The doe moved like lightning right at the exact moment it needed to, so my claws and fangs had missed their mark. *Lucky deer.* Or, more likely, a deer with an accomplice.

The wind shifted, and I got my answer. I'd never mistake that wolfie scent anywhere. Levi's deep-brown fur and soulful blue eyes came into my line of sight right where the doe had exited.

I huffed out a sigh, letting him know my annoyance. He'd stolen my kill. I shook myself off as I got up, taking the time to stretch my legs and pop the joints along my spine.

He yipped at me, his impatience clear, then, not waiting for a response, he bolted through the bushes, in the opposite direction from where the doe had gone.

I didn't want to follow him. I wasn't looking for company or a lecture about how I'd misused my power on the pack. I'd heard enough from Kane. His disappointment carried the weight of all three brothers.

Just as I was about to turn, run in the other direction and reject Levi's invitation, I caught a whiff of fire and ash and smoke, then of roasted meat. I swiveled my ears, hunting for the sound of Levi. There, not far ahead, was the crackling welcome I couldn't resist. It called me, one paw forward at a time, until I was pushing through leaves and branches.

"I already hunted," Levi said from his seat across the fire, knowing I was there before I'd even decided to show myself.

He didn't look up as I stepped through the underbrush, still in my wolf form.

"Felt like some wild meat cooked over a fire. Comfort food." He moved some logs with a stick, shifting them under the grate that held the steaming meat. "Wouldn't mind the company if you decide to stay."

I tilted my head, taking in the smells, the sounds, the way the fire moved, snapping up and reaching for the stars, licking the edges of the meat, sending smoke drifting toward the moon.

To my wolf, cooked meat was a poor substitute for a fresh, blood-soaked kill, but to my human side, Levi was right. This was comfort, not only the smell of food being cooked on an open fire but the memories it conjured — me with my uncle's ferals, a group of wolves I'd trained, sitting by a similar fire, cooking, drinking, laughing, bonding…sharing the wonders of the night.

A pang of regret, yearning for time long past, made me want to turn, walk away, find my own meal, but Levi made a sound, a low growl that rumbled from his chest. "You can't keep hiding from your truths, Charlie."

My truths? I was alone. Without family. Sold to the highest bidder. Destined to become a queen and hopelessly, forever trapped by my beast and my inability to control her actions.

"What happened wasn't your fault."

I shifted from wolf to human before his last word could fall, knowing that he was taking the stance I'd come to know him for…compassion, understanding.

"Like hell it wasn't." Like all werewolves, when I shifted, my clothes came with me, so I stepped out from the trees and into the clearing wearing yoga pants and a loose T-shirt. "I played with their minds. Can't take that truth away with your version of events."

Levi looked at me with patience in his eyes and a wry grin. "Yeah but at least I got you talking to me." He motioned to a log next to him. "Now that you're here, let's eat."

I shook my head, rolled my eyes, but did as he'd said. I was hungry, my stomach rumbling. As much as I wanted to atone for my sins against the Duke pack, I wouldn't do it with a food strike. That would for sure incite my beast's rage.

Sitting next to Levi, taking in the scent of his musk, knowing that hours ago we'd breached a boundary and kissed, only made me want to move closer when I should have wanted to move away. My armor was cracking. These men, these wolves? They'd captured a part of me that I'd locked up after my father had died.

He leaned forward, his arm brushing against my thigh, and I shivered. I wanted his comfort. I wanted to know that someone forgave me. *Why?* I'd never craved that kind of thing before. I was a lone wolf…strong, independent.

Lonely and alone.

"I…" Words crammed themselves in my throat. Apologetic, vulnerable words that wouldn't come out.

"First, we eat," Levi said as he handed me a hunk of meat on the tip of his knife. It dripped grease and blood, and the smell of herbs hit my nose and pulled a loud rumble from my belly. "Then we talk."

I met his eyes, nodded then took the offering.

Like everything I'd eaten made by Levi, the meat was soul-filling delicious. Even if I wanted to speak, I couldn't. My mouth was too busy. So, we ate in silence, staring at the fire, stealing glances at one another, satiating at least one of our needs. As my belly filled, longing took its place. I ached for Levi to move closer, to press himself against my arm, my thigh, to feel his touch, his heat. I tossed the remaining gristle and fat into the fire then wiped my mouth with the back of my hand, too unsure of where I stood with Levi to make a move, too self-conscious to open my mouth. I didn't really know how to apologize for what I'd done.

"You have some grease, right here," Levi said, his voice a rumbled whisper as he gently tilted my chin in his direction, rubbing his thumb along my cheek and the side of my lips. Our eyes met, and I saw a mirror of my own longing reflected back at me.

"Levi...I—"

He leaned in then kissed me, a take two of our first kiss, which had been interrupted by Kane in the library. This one went deeper, our tongues probing longer, harder, stroking the fire within my soul until my beast rattled her cage, and I was unsure if she wanted out to eat him or love him.

His hands were in my hair, tangled, digging his fingers into my scalp, pulling me closer, forcing me onto his lap where I fit so perfectly that I never wanted to leave. With my legs around his waist, my breasts teasing his chest, I slipped my hands around his back and rocked against the bulge in his pants.

He moaned, breaking our kiss to nuzzle into my throat, nipping teasingly as he pulled my head back, exposing the most vulnerable part of my body. My beast railed against her cage, but I shoved her into her pit, forcing her into the darkness so I could focus on what I wanted, what was right in front of me.

"Let me in."

Levi's voice echoed into my mind, against my conscious thoughts, knocking on the door of my barriers, the very ones holding my beast in place. I startled, tried to pull away from him, but he doubled down, increasing the pressure in my hair, holding me to him as he kissed me into oblivion.

"Charlie, call me to you." His voice vibrated against my walls, slithering past my armor.

I wanted to push him away...to fight against his intrusion.

But that was what had gotten me into a mess to begin with.

Quit fighting it, my traitorous mind whispered urgently.

Levi's chuckle against my lips told me he'd heard my inner thoughts, too.

I breathed out, sighing against his lips, letting my body go limp, the fight sliding out of me.

"Come to me, Levi."

Chapter Two

You swept into my waking dream world like a hurricane, enveloping me in your arms and taking us both down through the shadows of my mind, until we were floating in the ether.

No gravity to tug us, no shame or guilt to anchor us, we drifted, your lips to my lips, kissing me sweetly so all my thoughts were for you, in this moment, together.

I wanted to be naked with you and so we were. Clothes no longer a barrier to your skin.

In a space of nothingness, I felt your desire by the urgency of your touch, hands roving down my body, stroking along my flesh so it tingled, a wake of sparks left behind.

I also felt your longing, a twin to mine, coiling around me, infusing my veins with heat until my heart was beating in tune with yours.

I melted into your touch as you slipped your fingers along my slit, spreading me wide and making me moan against your lips. I writhed as you circled my clit, a slow tease of featherlight touches meant to coax the flame of my lust along with yours.

When you latched onto my nipple, your lips somehow leaving a trail along my skin at the same moment that you sucked and flicked my hard, aching nubs, I realized that time and space didn't matter in this reality. We were skin to skin and also not, our bodies rolling together and peeling apart. I could feel your fingers, your lips, your tongue in simultaneous places, touching, stroking, licking until my orgasm began to ricochet through each erogenous zone, building quickly.

"Levi," I gasped, arching my back when you slipped your fingers deep inside.

I felt powerful…in control. For the first time in my life, I felt like I could do what I wanted in this world. I wanted to touch you, to give you pleasure, too, the logistics of which hurt my brain – but it didn't matter because the space understood. Movement came swiftly, rotating us without breaking us apart, the shadows gently repositioning our bodies, giving me access to your cock where I could suck and stroke your dick with my mouth while you latched onto my clit with yours.

The ether of this world molded to my whims.

I took you down my throat, pressing my tongue against your shaft as I cupped your balls, gently massaging then pulling back, floating away from your dick so I could pump you properly, with both hands on your base and my lips around your tip. You shuddered, your legs shaking, like you were restraining yourself, holding back. I knew the feeling. I wanted to draw this out, too, pull every second of pleasure from you as you lapped at my pussy, delving deep with your tongue and fingers, sucking hard on my clit.

I let us roll, switching us from top to bottom again and again, the shadows pulling us along their current, not caring about anything but you, your salty flesh making my mouth water, your pulsing cock vibrating in my mouth. Threads of connection bound us in place, tying us together so we were one, flesh to flesh. This time, I wasn't scared. This wasn't like when I'd cast a net around the pack wolves, forcing them into a fight with their instincts. This was more of a mutual fusion. Your threads weaving with mine, your essence melding into me.

This was how it was supposed to be. A mutual awakening. Painless, gentle, making a bond that comforted and, in this case, that also stoked my flaming lust to an inferno.

My orgasm came like a lightning strike, full force, flashes across my eyes, sparks flying and pleasure forking along every nerve, every synapse, until I was shuddering and shaking. You followed close behind, spewing your load down my throat as I greedily sucked and licked until you stopped groaning.

The shadows pulled us apart as we came undone by our climax, then put us back together, me in your arms, you holding me tight. Nestled and cocooned, I felt light. I felt happy.

Chapter Three

Levi

We were lying on the forest floor, satiated, our bellies full, our bodies slick with sweat quickly cooling in the early morning air.

It was hard to tell if we'd pleasured each other in the real world. My body bore the aftereffects of sex play with Charlie, my heart thudding, blissed out in a buzz, but we weren't in this world when we'd come together, and in the past, when we'd been intimate, I'd woken to the same sensations — satisfaction, happiness, love.

"It felt different this time." Charlie's warm breath cascaded over my chest where her head rested in the crook of my shoulder. Her hand was draped lazily across my abdomen.

I could lie like this with her forever. All to myself. Us alone.

"You let it be a two-way connection." I kissed the top of her head, taking a chance that our intimacy extended to right now. "It felt right, don't you think?"

She was quiet for a heartbeat or two, maybe wondering if she wanted to stay like this with me. I tried not to panic. I hoped she'd felt what I had. I hoped she felt the rightness of us being like this. I hoped it was finally sinking in that she could open herself to me, to us — my brothers and me. We wouldn't hurt her.

"It felt like these threads were weaving us together, and when we connected like that, it amped up what was already there — my power, I mean. It tied everything together so I could control things better." She paused, letting a slow breath out that tickled my sensitive nipples. "It's hard to explain."

"No, I think I get it. I add turbo to your engine."

"Sure, something like that." She laughed at my ridiculous analogy. "I guess that's what the scrolls have been telling us. Right? I mean, that's what they seem to be saying."

"If it feels right, then I think we're on to something." I tried for a nonchalant shrug when she lifted her head to look at me, her brow furrowed and hair tumbled over her shoulders.

"You don't know?" She quirked a smile, her lips twitching just a little. "I thought you were some kind of genius about our history."

I brushed her hair back, so grateful for the chance to be intimate with Charlie like this. "This is all new to me, too, Charlie, and the scrolls don't tell a full story."

She slumped a bit. *Thinking, always thinking. Or more like, always doubting.*

"But I believe that this is the way it's supposed to be between a queen and her mates." I touched her collarbone. "I feel like we've unlocked something. I feel like this is just the beginning for us."

"A beginning for us?" She pulled herself back like I'd said something to frighten her. By the hard expression on her face, I realized I'd tread into dangerous commitment territory. "What about the prophecy, your brothers?"

Damn, she thought I was trying to keep her to myself—which, to be honest, I'd love to do. "This isn't me making a move to lock you down, Charlie. I know I can't keep you to myself. I know you don't belong to any man. I do think you should explore your connection to Kane and Johnny. Let them in like you've let me in. See what comes of it." I swallowed the lump in my throat. "You never know... You might find what you're looking for."

She pulled away from me completely, her frown firmly in place. *Fuck,* I wanted to kick myself for being so pushy and ending our intimacy.

She reached for her discarded T-shirt, which was lying tangled in a bush to our left, then slipped it on. Her panties and yoga pants quickly followed. I mourned the loss and cursed my stupid mouth.

It fascinated me that our clothes seemed to strip themselves off in her dream world and apparently in the real world at her whim, but when we shifted, they stayed where they needed to be, ready for us to transform back to human, fully clothed.

It made me want to explore the limitlessness of her powers. What could she do if she put her mind to something?

Now, of course, was not the time...

"I don't know what this means." She motioned between the two of us. "But I'm not looking for something. I'm not missing a part of me or longing to be complete." That lie must have tasted rotten on her tongue. Her loneliness radiated through our newly formed connections. "I know I'm not ready for whatever commitment you all seem to want from me."

When she took a seat on the log, I realized I hadn't scared her away. *At least there's that.* With a reluctant grunt, I got up from my bed of leaves then put my clothes on, too.

"I don't know if you ever met my stepmother, Luca. She was my father's first wife." Charlie poked at what was left of the fire with a stick, coaxing it back to flame with a few quick breaths. "My father always had romantic notions about heroism. When Luca's husband died protecting my dad, he'd felt obligated to show his loyalty and gratitude by marrying her, adopting her sons, treating them as his own. I know you know it's not unusual for that to happen in legacy families." She gave me a look that made it seem okay for me to take my seat next to her once again. "He devoted himself to making her happy, to being a replacement father to my stepbrothers. She wanted a child with him, but he put the pack first, fixated on building it into what it is today." She sighed. "From what he told me over the years and what I've pieced together, he was satisfied with that arrangement, content to be a husband and stepfather, not interested in having his own child, until he met my mother."

"Then he understood real love," I guessed. Having never heard this backstory before, I couldn't help but wonder what Charlie's childhood would have been like with a stepmother who had been set aside for a second wife, one who was the recipient of the alpha's love.

She nodded, her gaze riveted on the fire that had gone back to smoldering.

"When Kane told me that Sal killed my mother—" She sucked in a sharp breath then let it slide out slowly. "I didn't understand at first. Why? Why would Sal do such a thing? But deep down I think I knew. My mother had always been a symbol of betrayal to my stepbrothers, and I was a product of that betrayal. So, it makes sense to me now why Sal wanted my mother dead, why he wants me dead, too."

"He doesn't want you dead. He wants you to suffer." I touched her cheek so she'd look at me. "He wants you to feel humiliated, to be dominated by Kane. He wants you to know that he has power over you."

"If I mate with you, with Kane and Johnny, won't I be giving him what he wants?" She rubbed her hands over her arms like she was cold.

I took the stick from her hand then got to work banking the fire up once again.

"He's not expecting us to be in love." I held up a hand when she started to argue. "I'm not saying I'm in love with you, Charlie." *But I am, fuck. I'm totally lost to her.* "What I'm saying is that your stepbrother has no idea what bonding with us will do to your already immense power. He won't see you coming when you decide to get the revenge you're owed."

Her eyes sparked, and her frown faded. Deep down, I knew, she was terrified of giving up control, while at the same time wanting so badly to be a part of a pack. It didn't take our connection to understand that. Every wolf wanted to be part of something bigger. It was in our nature. For Charlie, though, being part of a harem, even if she was the one uniting us all, meant danger, just like it had for her mother.

"I'm saying that letting me in was the first step, and it could be all you need to beat that bastard down and put him in his place. Connections with me, Johnny, Kane — not our bite — could be all the catalyst you need to get what you deserve." I touched her hand, coaxing her to twine her fingers with mine. "I don't know what all this means, but I'm telling you, it feels right and, in my genius mind" — I nudged her shoulder so she swayed — "that means we're doing what we're destined to be doing. Even if we don't mate, even if I never bite you, the connection I feel with you now? It's something important."

She looked down at our fingers then lifted our hands to her chest and laid it over her heart. "It scares me to death, Levi, but I think you're right."

Chapter Four

Johnny

"There's only one way this is going to go." I slipped my arm into the crook of hers and tugged her toward the backyard where the boys were waiting. "The pack wants retribution."

Charlie attempted to dig her heels in, and I had a brief but powerful reminder of her werebeast lying in wait for any reason to rip my throat out. She yanked us both back.

"Relax... It's a dodgeball game." I locked eyes with her and tried for my best be-cool expression. "We do it every Sunday."

"Dodgeball," she said, incredulously.

"Werewolf style." I got her walking again. "No werebeasts allowed."

"Which is why this is a terrible idea." She didn't attempt to stop our progress, though. "I don't want to beast out when everyone is having fun."

"You won't." Because I'd figured out the secret to calming her beast. It wasn't just the neck hold that had subdued her the other day in the forest but what I'd been saying to her. Whispering in her ear must have gotten the message through that we weren't a threat, because the beast had finally let Charlie go — or, at least, that was what I was telling myself. I hadn't debriefed with my brothers, but I'd like to think I had a connection with Charlie that maybe her beast was starting to accept. I'd definitely felt connected to her, in her head, if only because I'd felt her desperately trying to regain control. It was in her tense muscles and rumbling growl. Even as her werebeast side was tearing my arm to shreds, I knew Charlie was in there fighting to get out. I suspected her werebeast heard me and took heed.

Or we just got lucky, and the neck hold had worked.

"You don't know that." She let me lead, which showed just how nervous she was to face the pack. I got it, I did, but this was the only way she was going to redeem herself, and I knew she knew it. "I'm surprised they'll even let me on the field with them."

"They love to show off, especially to females." It wasn't a lie. Although I did have to promise them a night at the pub with all-you-could-eat wings to get them to agree to a game including Charlie after what had happened with her attempted mind meld.

Kane still hadn't made an appearance from his wing of the mansion, and I knew it was because he was fuming over what Charlie had done. When he was super pissed, he isolated himself until he cooled down. It was a strategy that had kept him from doing a lot of unwise shit over the years. His temper was unreal... kind of similar to what Charlie's werebeast was like.

Her werebeast, like it was a separate entity. Levi would have my head if he knew I was thinking that way. He and Kane both thought Charlie had split herself in three. Three separate entities—her wolf, herself and her werebeast. She should be all in one, a package deal, but somewhere along the way she developed some not-so-great coping mechanisms, and Levi thought it was all because of those masters that had trained her. Kane agreed. Me? I could appreciate her struggle. Sometimes I'd like to shove my wolf side away and just be human, blend in, be normal. How tempting would it be to silence the ever-pulsing desire of my wolfie needs? Shelter. Food. Mate. Persistent urges to secure all three all the time.

Charlie being here had quieted some of that instinct, cementing my belief that she was the one. She was mine. I just needed her to see that I was hers.

I knew Levi had made some headway with her. Not that he'd said anything to me but the shit-eating grin he'd been wearing all day had said it all. He'd felt he'd conquered her in some way, and his ego was glowing.

And that alone was enough to get my competitive drive to triple. Charlie wasn't a prize, but if mega-geek Levi could get her to melt, then so could I.

Charlie didn't say anything else until we were stepping onto the multi-purpose field. The guys were all playing around, tossing the ball, doing their best to ignore us. I could tell their hackles were up since the tension on the field doubled. It made my skin tight and the urge to shift very real.

Charlie kept walking until she was standing center, looking small in the middle of the pack. The guys all stopped what they were doing, finally forced to accept that she was going to get up in their faces. There were low murmurs, some growls, grumbles but they turned toward her, willing to listen at least.

"I know I did you wrong, and I'm sorry." Charlie projected her voice as she scanned the guys, making eye contact with as many as she could.

Pride swelled in my chest. I hadn't been expecting her to own up like this…to stick her neck out.

"I made a mistake. It hadn't been my intention to trap you like I did. I meddled with power I don't understand, and you all paid for it. I'll never forgive myself for that, and I don't expect you to, either."

No one spoke. Charlie's cheeks flared red. Her obvious discomfort sat in my chest like a boulder, empathy to the extreme. I wanted to save her, but I held steady, soaking up the tension. She nodded, accepting the silence as something other than forgiveness—or at least affirmation of whatever was going on in her head. She turned to go. I was about to give *the look* to the pack, the one that said, 'cut her some slack'. I hadn't coached them to hear her out, but I had expected more flexibility.

"Everyone makes mistakes," one of the guys in the back said—probably Lewis, if I were to guess. He was always the first to forgive and forget.

"No judgment here," another added. "We were all a bunch of fuck-ups when we joined."

"You still are, Steve."

The whole group laughed, someone threw a ball and it knocked one of the guys on his ass. That was when Charlie must have realized we played with weighted balls. She barked a laugh. Another ball flew, and just like that, the game was on.

Charlie, being in the middle, was caught up in the melee, and I dove in next to her. The teams were quickly sorted by skins and wolves. We were on skins, remaining in our human forms with one huge exception...Charlie's ability to partially shift.

"Show these guys what you can do, Charlie!" I roared as I caught a ball mid-air, absorbing the weight before zinging it back to the sender.

She managed to jump out of the way of a ball that skimmed her head but didn't use her shifting abilities to aid our team.

I psyched out a wolf with a fake throw then tossed the ball Charlie's way for the hit. She barely caught the heavy thing, swaying backward as she fumbled it for another member of our team to snatch and deliver.

"Charlie, you can use your unique talents, you know." I rolled my eyes when she looked at me blankly. "Shift your arms or something."

"That's cheating!" she said as she shook her head.

Three balls came her way in quick succession, and she turned to face them, shifting instinctively, her powerful wolf legs getting her out of the way in a seamless duck, dive then capture. She hauled back two of the balls, one in each clawed hand then sent them reeling, taking out two members of the other team.

"Hell yes!" I yelled, and the rest of the team cheered.

Being able to shift parts of her body was an element of who she was, and it was time for her to accept it.

The guys pumped her up, shouting her name, throwing balls her way just to see what she could do. As team members fell, struck out one after another, Charlie kept the game going. Her energy was infectious, and her laughter ignited chortles all over the field, even a few yips from the wolves who weren't on our team.

I was so in awe and so caught up in her magnificence that I took a hit to the chest that sent me sprawling. I was out, but Charlie kept going.

* * * *

She'd cleared the field in record time, and when we'd switched sides and our team had become the wolves, she'd done it again—kicking ass all over the place and impressing me more and more.

She hadn't won over the guys yet, but she would. I knew it.

"We pay a premium on nights like tonight," I said as we walked into the Knight and Armor Pub. "I laid down a generous flat rate because these monsters can eat."

"Don't forget the booze!" Steve and Rue walked by and slapped my back, laughing about how much money they thought it cost for a night out. They had no idea. Kane was going to blast me when he got the bill. I grinned. I felt it was my brotherly duty to test his limits. What good was money if it wasn't used for some fun?

"I notice it's only us here." Charlie, observant as always, scanned the noisy bar. "You bought the whole place out, didn't you?"

"Like I said, a premium is paid." I shrugged as I weaved us around the tables, each brimming with high energy and wicked cheer. "These guys deserve the best, but I don't want them hooking up with a bunch of local women for one-night stands. That's how accidents happen."

"Accidents like mauling?" Charlie sounded doubtful as she surveyed the guys, her frown showing she couldn't imagine the pack doing anything so barbaric. I was relieved to see that she didn't lump us in with the types of ferals that caused *that* kind of trouble wherever they went.

"No, nothing like that." I waved the bartender over. "Just broken hearts and drama, more trouble than it's worth. The guys can date, hook up, whatever. They just need to do it out of our territory."

"You mean, stir up shit in other territories." Charlie laughed then leaned in and asked for a local craft beer.

She smelled amazing, like cinnamon and clove, peppermint, maybe vanilla. I wanted to nuzzle her throat and breathe her in. It was more than a primal urge. She was familiar in ways she shouldn't be yet. I knew that had to be a result of the time we'd spent together in her dreams. I wished I could remember the last three years, but I was going to trust my gut and say we were close in her unconscious realm. *Very* close.

I needed to figure out how to cross that intimacy into the real world.

"We all have urges," I said as I reined myself in, noting the irony in my words where Charlie was concerned and motioned to the bartender for what Charlie was having. "And none of the guys has overstepped too badly."

"So, no major turf wars over women." Charlie clinked glasses with me. "Yet."

"Exactly." I lifted my pint.

"Hey, Charlie, come play a game." Tre waved a pool cue our way. "Show us what you've got."

I wanted to keep her by my side and hog her to myself, but the whole point of this night was to get her in with the boys, to make more than peace. I wanted her entrenched. I wanted her heart to melt for each member of the pack. Not in a sexual way, I wasn't that into free love, but in a committed-to-the-clan way.

"It's going to be one competition after another now." I laughed. "Hey, Charlie, wing-eating contest. Show us what you can do. Hey, Charlie, beer-guzzling contest…"

She rolled her eyes and smacked my chest playfully before snatching up her beer, guzzling it in two deep pulls then slamming the glass down on the bar.

"They have no idea what I can do," she said as she beelined for the pool table, cracking her knuckles along the way.

I'm in love.

More than I already had been, that was.

Chapter Five

Charlie

I knew what Johnny was up to, and even though I wanted to hate it, rebel against the obvious push to bond with these guys, I didn't. I was having too much fun. Being part of a pack, even on the periphery, was a homecoming I hadn't expected.

I knew there was tension still, a mistrust of me and worry that I might use my mind-meld fuckery again, but I was determined to prove that I wouldn't betray them twice. I liked these guys. They were rough and tumble ferals with hearts on their sleeves and seemed ready for fun and games, the same as what my uncle's ferals had been like. As much as that realization made my heart heavy, it also gave me a zing of hope. This might be a second chance for me to redeem myself — to become part of a pack, aligned with them, one of the guys. It was something I hadn't thought I'd missed, but the hole in my heart was bubbling with all kinds of hope, and I kinda loved it.

Just like Levi had said, I didn't have to take a bite to be part of a pack. I just had to bend a knee and swear loyalty — palm to palm, a self-inflicted bite mark to seal the deal in blood. I'd never done it, of course, I was born into a powerful clan, but the idea of selecting a family, a new start with these guys? Well, it thawed my fears to the possibilities.

That, and maybe I'd call Johnny and Kane into my subconscious awareness, just like I'd done with Levi. No, not maybe…definitely. I needed to bond in some way with the boys and quit pushing them away like I'd been doing. At least then, maybe, they'd accept that I wanted to be part of the pack without me taking a mating bite from any of them.

In no way did I want to lead the pack, dominate them or demand their loyalty as anything other than a member. It sounded like a good plan to me, but would Kane accept my pledge rather than my submission as a mate? Would he, Levi and Johnny be cool with me being a soldier instead of an alpha? Maybe a 'member with benefits' kind of deal?

I looked at the guys surrounding me, laughing, walloping each other on the back, telling jokes at one another's expense. I wanted to be part of this…a member of the pack. There to kick Sal's ass but not leading the charge.

Yeah, that was what felt right.

It would probably piss Kane off, though…not getting his way.

Hmmm… I smiled. Yeah, I liked the feeling of that, too.

"She's hustlin' us, boys!" Vic waved his glass around, sloshing whiskey down his shirt. "And drinking us under the table, too!"

Not sure if kicking these guys' asses at pool was the way to go, but I sure as shit wasn't going to let them win just to save some egos. *Fuck that.*

I smirked and shrugged. "Don't tell me you've never been hustled before." I put a hand on my hip. "The way you play pool, Victor, I'd bet you're used to losing your shirt."

The crowd *ohh*ed, and a few guys slapped Vic on the back, laughing.

"Love your shit-talk, girl." Lex slammed a wad of cash down on the pool table. "I'm putting fifty on Charlie making this next shot."

"I'm in on that bet." A few other guys stepped up and put more bills down.

The pressure was real. I eyed the next shot. Not exactly an easy one but, if I made it, I was in the clear to win...again.

I fished out a bill from my pocket and threw it down, too.

The crowd went wild — whoops, yells, cheers, lots of backslapping.

I leaned down, got nice and close to the felt, adjusted my cue, sucked in a deep breath, held it, then made the shot and prayed to the werewolf gods that I didn't miss.

The ball curved left, spinning just like I intended, hit the red then the yellow, and sank them both.

Yes!

Thundering cheers roared around me. Someone patted my shoulders. Another someone squeezed my arm. I got a bunch of high fives as I made my way to the last shot. "Eight ball side pocket." I took aim. "Double or nothing."

Another round of *ohhhs*, *ahhhs* and a whole lot of whistling happened, but I didn't wait for them to calm down and instead capitalized on their energy. The eight ball sank. The crowd went wild.

Beer sloshed everywhere. Shots arrived on several trays. I got handed two tequilas, which would make me gag, but there was no way I was turning it down. The warm fuzzies I was feeling in my stomach had nothing to do with the alcohol and everything to do with the comradery. This was how it had been with my uncle's ferals. We'd laughed. We'd played. We'd hung out.

As I double-fisted the shots, banging them back one after another and grinned through the burn, I realized that the secret to connecting with that pack so long ago was because of the down time we had together just as much as the training we'd endured. Those guys had been my guys. They'd welcomed me, considered me one of them. They'd embraced me, and damn, I missed that kind of connection. The lone wolf life appealed in a lot of ways, but there was something to be said for Friday night fun with a pack.

With my uncle's ferals, it had been campfires and nights sleeping under the stars, collecting in a heap, cuddling for body heat, our fur nestled in together, hearing one another's heartbeats and deep snores. We'd spent weeks in the mountains, training, playing, hunting, being wolves together then coming back for fire-cooked meals that satisfied our human sentimentalities.

I missed those guys. They were good. Rough around the edges, sure, but inherently good.

A pang of guilt rocked me faster than the tequila. My grin faltered. If I kept going with these guys—Kane's pack—if I kept infiltrating their defenses, I'd destroy them, too.

The thought sobered me enough to want escape. The fantasy I'd conjured moments before popped, and I knew it was an impossible dream. Not only would Kane refuse to accept my pledge to be one of the guys, but the closer I also got to this crew, the more chance there would be for me to bring about their untimely deaths.

Nope. Not going to do that again.

I needed some air. Time to clear my head and get out from under all the comforting testosterone.

I took two steps back, extracting myself from the throng, who were distracted by new platters heaped with wings and a few symbolic veggies. I turned right into Johnny's solid wall of a chest and nearly collapsed against him, momentarily dizzy from the quick swivel and sudden stop.

He smelled of all manly musk and tantalizing wolf. He had his hands on my hips, and I looked up into his silver eyes.

"You did good," he said, his voice husky and his eyes full of what I thought might be pride.

And that kicked me right in the gut. It was good until it wasn't—until it was blood and guts and death all around me.

"I need some air," I managed to choke out.

His expression wobbled, a frown pulling his eyebrows down. "All okay?"

"I will be." There was no point in lying. "Just tripped into the past for a second. It hurts. This..."—I waved my hand around—"confuses me."

Johnny nodded, then slid his hand down my arm and wrapped his fingers around mine. He was all warmth and strength, and I curled my fingers between his, locking in as if it were normal to hold hands with him.

"There's a secret patio out back," he said quickly, turning then tugging me behind him, and any further words were swallowed by the white noise of fifty wolves having a great time around us.

I noted how Johnny made eye contact with a few guys as we passed. They nodded, slithered curious looks my way then moved on to other things.

We exited the main room via a partially hidden hallway that I thought was not for customers until I saw a door marked *Smoking Lounge*.

"We won't be bothered here." Johnny pushed open the door then guided me through.

I guessed no one in the pack smoked.

Or more likely, Johnny had sent a message as we walked back here together, and everyone knew not to disturb us.

I didn't know how to feel about that. I knew expectations were running high. Despite my thoughts just a few minutes before, I was nervous to cross a line with yet another Duke brother.

The patio was decorated with fake plants and ratty couches, but it was secluded and cozy. There was a breeze from the ocean, and my senses opened to take it in.

I closed my eyes, inhaled, let the cleansing air pick up the pieces of my guilt and float them away. *Ha. Right.* As if it were that easy. My shame was like a crazy glue, stuck with no hope of ever unlatching. I let my breath go then looked up at Johnny.

He was wafting all kinds of concerned vibes as he led me to the couch.

"Hitting a little close to home, right?" He didn't let my hand go as we both collapsed to the surprisingly plush seats.

"Yeah, I mean, I've been here before." I waved my hand around. "Not literally, obviously."

"No, I get it." Johnny leaned close, nudging my shoulder. "You're full of heart, Charlie…even if you don't want us to see it."

I snorted in response but stifled the urge to rub my chest as if I could ease the pain in my heart from that alone.

"As much as I know you're hitting on some nerves from your past, it means you're connecting with the guys, and that's what I think needs to happen."

It didn't take a genius to know that was what he was after by including me in today's events. He probably had no idea just what ripping this particular scab off was doing to me, the turmoil of wanting so badly to form attachments while at the same time being terrified that I'd ruin everything again.

"I get it. What you're trying to do, I mean."

He laughed, looking at me with a cocked eyebrow. "Oh, really?"

"It's not going to work," I lied. "I won't let you all in." I thumped my chest with my fist. "Been there, done that."

"Hey, give me some credit." He raised his hands. "I'm not a big move kinda guy. I like to take things slow. Slide in softly. Ease the defenses down." He lifted his arm, stretching wide, then laid his forearm along my shoulders.

"Very smooth." I laughed.

He tapped my chin with two fingers, slowly tilting my head up and to the side. I locked eyes with him, a familiarity there that unnerved me.

"My only intention for tonight was to do this." He looked at my lips, his eyes hooded, then leaned in.

I couldn't stop him. I didn't want to. It was a bandage for my wound, and I needed it.

He kissed me tenderly, slowly, lips pressed to lips, body heat activated, tingling running over my scalp and down my chest. He took it slow, just like he said he would. Moving closer. Pulling me in.

I opened my mouth to him, granting him access. A fissure opening somewhere deep as my dream life became real life, and his kiss held the passion and possession it always did.

"Johnny," I breathed as he pulled back, forehead to my forehead. "I don't want to hurt you."

"You won't." His tone was so earnest, so sure. He pressed into me, kissing like he was the oxygen I needed.

No matter what he said, I knew what I was capable of, and I knew the people around me weren't safe, so long as my beast lived within.

Chapter Six

You didn't come to me tonight. None of you did. I was lonely…craving company. I'd had too much tequila and your scent, Johnny, was in the ether, surrounding me, coating my skin. I could still taste you in my mouth, tracks of your kisses still ghosted along my skin.

I had too many thoughts in my head. Doubts. Guilt. Uncertainty. I wanted someone to blow them all away.

I was stuck. I needed to make a decision. I should go home, resume my solitary life away from any pack. Be a lone wolf. Cut my losses and be grateful for my freedom.

But, who was I kidding? I was past that point. With you. With Levi.

Instead of dreaming any of you into existence, I scrolled through our shared history. Levi, your pure heart and soulful eyes brought comfort and peace, security. Johnny, your silver glint excited me, revved me up, made me want to take risks. To throw myself out there. Open myself up.

Kane…I wanted you. I wanted to know what it felt like to kiss you in real life. I was afraid of how much I wanted that.

But did I want you enough to take your bite? To choose you over the others?

I knew the offer was there. Why have one when I could have three?

Three bites were three too many.

I couldn't be under your control. I couldn't be tied to you for eternity.

I couldn't survive what would happen when I destroyed you all.

What you were asking was not about loyalty, submission or love. It was about survival – yours and mine.

I was the only one thinking about the end of the fairy tale. What happened when my beast decided the story was over?

What I wanted was your touch. I wanted Levi to caress a line along my hip, gentle fingers moving to ignite my passion.

I wanted Johnny's lips kissing a tract across my collarbone, down the center of my chest, teasingly close to my tits but not quite scratching that itch.

I wanted Kane's fingers digging into my scalp, tugging my hair as he swallowed my moans, kissing me until I lost my breath.

You would spread my thighs, featherlight tickling along the crevasse of my ass cheeks, using thumbs to slide along my folds then open me up. You'd stare at me, your liquid-silver eyes piercing me like a cock, your hot gaze making me writhe with anticipation.

You'd lick my nipples, taking one, then the other into the heat of your mouth. You'd be attentive to both, flicking and licking, pinching and rolling, simultaneous torture.

You'd stretch my lips wide, offering your dick, watching me take you down, your molten stare scorching me when you nudged the gate of my throat, and I released all resistance then swallowed you whole.

You'd rub my clit, rolling the pad of your thumb over and over, spearing me with your fingers, stroking my G-spot so I arched up, begging with my body for more.

Sensations would overwhelm me, flood my body with your attention, rotating along my awareness, caught in the fog of my dream world so I wouldn't know who was touching my pussy, who was licking my clit or my nipples and who was slowly guiding their cock between my lips.

You'd be relentless, stoking my orgasm to its peak, holding me in place as I chased the high I knew was coming. You'd touch every erogenous zone, plucking the most sensitive nerves until I was writhing, moaning, roaring through a cascading wave of pleasure, not wanting it to stop, lost in the bliss of all three of you worshipping me.

I wanted you all. Not for an eternity... I didn't deserve that. No, I wanted you for this slice of time, and that was unfair to all of you.

Chapter Seven

Kane

I'd asked Charlie to meet me on the field once again. This time, I invited Levi and Johnny to join us — not because I wanted an audience or to spike my competitive urges, but because I had a plan. Charlie needed to stabilize her selves — the sides of her that she was taught to separate. The wolf, the beast, they should be melded. Those masters weakened her. On purpose? Some grand design to keep her under the thumb of the patriarchy? My gut said no. They did it because they were scared for her, of her...who knew? Her father wanted her to be the strongest female. I bet he didn't have any clue that he was paying for her to be hobbled. I planned to fix that today — or at least get things started.

"Just because I'm walking here of my own free will doesn't mean I'm green lighting any torture from you today." Her words were sharp, but the curl of her lips told me she didn't hate my heavy-handed approach. She definitely hadn't hated my form of punishment the other night in her dreams.

She was wearing gray spandex shorts, like a second skin that showcased her killer ass, and a loose tank that highlighted the definition in her arms and shoulders. Her cleavage was peeking at the neckline, plush pillows of flawless skin that I wanted to sink into and bury my face completely. Seeing her naked in her dream the other night—a dream that I remembered, *thank fuck*—was enough to send me to my knees. Luckily, I had sense enough to stand my ground. She needed a firm hand, and I had a message to send.

She was lean yet voluptuous, and the clothes she was wearing today were a tease. I wanted to strip her bear, touch her in real life, possess her completely.

As if reading my mind, she swayed her hips as she closed the distance to me.

Minx.

I licked my lips before I met her eyes boldly, letting her know exactly what I was thinking.

"As I've said to you before, when you're in my realm, you'll do as I say."

She stopped right in front of me, and I couldn't help myself. I closed the space so I was looming, a fraction of an inch away from her. She smelled like lavender today...citrus, too. It made my mouth water. She looked up at me with an almost defiant tilt to her face, her chin jutting, lips quirking.

I knew she was thinking about her dream, wondering if I remembered how I'd punished her. I wanted to keep her guessing, but something sparked in her eyes and her cheeks flushed to a pretty pink.

"Am I in for more punishment today?" She held my stare, and her pupils dilated. She bit down, tiny fangs poking into the cushion of her plush bottom lip.

My knees went weak. I wanted to fall on top of her, ravage her with my mouth, my hands. Every part of my body screamed to touch her.

She sucked in a shallow breath, her body so close that I could almost feel the press of her tits to my chest.

"You got off easy." My voice grumbled like a freight train. My cock strained against my shorts. "And I'm not done with you. Not even close."

Her heart ramped up. I could hear it like thunder in my ears. She nodded, acceptance mixed with excitement? Hard to tell. She could be biding her time before ripping my throat out.

"We've tried this your way. We've slowed things down. We've given you time. It's not working, and you can't seem to stop yourself from being reckless."

She opened her mouth like she was actually going to argue with me. Her lips formed an O. What would she say? It was one mistake? One time?

"It was one too many, and it won't happen again," I said.

She clamped her mouth shut. Her eyes blazed, widened like she had a lot to say but was biting her tongue. I knew she liked to argue back. I knew my brothers wouldn't mind that. In fact, I knew they'd let her get away with a lot. Indulged her. Encouraged the sass.

That wasn't my way.

My brothers had made headway with her. She'd let them in while she'd kept me out. Maybe it was because I'd been so brutal with her, but someone had to be. *And she knows it.*

I reached up and snaked my fingers into her ponytail, tangled myself in her thick hair. "You'll do as I say, no argument."

She blinked hard, her lips parted, small pants exploding from her lungs. Sweat beaded along her throat. It was hot out here, the sun scorching already, a rare heat wave to hit Vancouver. It was a fucking blessing on skin like Charlie's. I watched a trickle of moisture move along her chest, meandering in ways that I wanted to.

"Kane," she whispered, wincing when I wrenched her head to the side.

I lowered my mouth to the heat of her skin, inhaling her scent, letting it play along my tongue.

She swayed closer, her body brushing against mine, but she kept her hands at her side, seeming to await my commands.

"I know you've been with my brothers. I know you've let them touch you...taste you." I ran my lips with a whispered kiss along the trail of dampness. Goosebumps raised along her throat. Her pulse pounded below the surface. My mouth ached, fangs ready to punch through. The only time a male could partially transform was for the mating bite, and I felt the pressure of that need like a volcano ready to go off. She swallowed, hard, her muscles straining as I kept her head at an angle. "I will have you, Charlotte."

She shivered. I held her there, breathed in her desire. Her mind might have been torn, unsure of what move to make, but her body wasn't.

I let her go, giving her the space to stagger back in time for Levi to make it to the top of the hill.

"Sorry, I'm late. I was reading up on a few things. Checking my notes." He stopped abruptly, taking us both in. My heaving chest, clenched fists, my failure to calm myself back to normal. Charlie, her face flushed, moved a few steps back as she lifted her fingers to her throat, tracing the exact path my lips had taken moments before.

"All okay here?" Levi was worried I was still mad at Charlie. It was clear on his face — the furrowed brows, the nervous twitch of his cheek. He was a powerhouse in his own rite, but he knew how I could get when I was pissed, and he certainly wouldn't know the difference between passion and anger when he saw it…where I was concerned, anyway.

"Charlie and I were just getting on the same page again." I turned my back to both of them, using the move to take in some deep breaths as I walked toward the middle of the field. "We'll start with some drills to warm up."

Johnny was late, as usual.

Charlie groaned.

I shot her a glare that cut her sound off abruptly.

She's learning.

"Yeah, right…same page. Sure." Levi snorted. "You two are going to need to sync up if this is going to work."

"If *what* is going to work?" Charlie, finally finding her voice again, pulled her focus away from me then turned to Levi.

"You didn't fill her in yet?" Levi scoffed at me when I shrugged.

I had more important things to get straight with her first.

"Charlie, we know you're not interested in taking our marks." Levi was excited by his theory, his voice pumped, words flowing quickly. "And you're right. It's an archaic practice. I think I've figured out a work around so you can step into your role—"

"Whoa!" Charlie lifted a hand. "You're still set on me becoming alpha?"

Levi's eyes widened. "The prophecy—"

"The prophecy that says I belong to you?" Charlie scoffed and crossed her arms.

"The prophecy that says you belong *with* us."

Levi was smooth, I'd give him that.

I'd have stuck to blunt and clear. Yes, the prophecy said she'd rise up, take the bites of powerful wolves to bolster her. I planned to be one of those who bonded with her.

"Okay, what's the difference?"

"The difference is, maybe we can find a way to make the mental link more in sync." Levi motioned to me. "We talked and realized that when your beast took over the other day, all three of us tried in one way or another to coax you back down using our connections to you. Kane tried physically. Johnny says he tried using his words, in your head."

Her eyes widened. "I thought that was you," she blurted, looking at me.

"You heard my voice in your head?" I'd been semi-conscious, with it enough to know what was going on but her beastly head had knocked some stars into mine. Had I been trying to communicate with her? It was possible on some subconscious level, yes, but I wasn't intentionally trying to do anything but stay in the moment.

"I heard whispering, I just thought... I mean, it sounded like you." She shook her head then waved Levi on. "Never mind."

Did it bother her? That we were gaining access to her mind? She'd heard us, felt us, yearned for us, and in her mind, we were clearly one in the same. That was a good sign for our plans. It meant, at some level, her mind and body were accepting our role in her future.

"I used a visual connection," Levi said, darting his gaze from her to me then back again. "I was trying to get you to focus on my face."

"And your voice," she said. "You were talking. I couldn't hear your words, but I knew you were trying to calm me down. The cadence of your voice... It was soothing."

By the way she shifted her eyes down and shuffled her feet, I could tell admitting that made her uncomfortable. We were getting to her...in one way or another.

"What'd I miss?" Johnny came running onto the field, his hair in a topknot and dressed in his gym clothes.

"I'm just filling Charlie in on things."

"Levi's got a good plan, right?" Johnny rubbed his hands together, practically bouncing on his toes. "Totally going to work."

"I haven't gotten there yet." Levi scratched at the scruff on his jaw. "As I was saying, it's clear that we each have a connection with you."

There was a new flush to her cheeks as Johnny took in her appearance, lingering longer than necessary on her legs in her spandex.

"So, what we propose is that you let the beast side out, then we work together, all four of us, to reintegrate *her* with the rest of you."

Charlie opened her mouth, but Levi kept going.

"We'll act as your anchors, keeping you focused while you work on latching the threads you have with us to that side of you, too."

"How in the hell do you think I'll be able to do that?" Charlie threw her hands up, clearly exasperated.

"How did the masters teach you to separate those parts of yourself?" I took a step closer, wanting to be part of the conversation, even if it wasn't my theory we were exploring. I hadn't endorsed it with my full heart, but with only one other idea, an extreme one, I was willing to give it a try.

She seemed to be thinking, her face tilted up to the sun, her eyes closed. "They taught me to build a leash, then a cage." She squinted as she lowered her face. "It took months of conditioning, years of constant practice. Obviously, I'm still trying to master it."

"Because it's against your natural state," Levi said. "Does she ever come out in your dreams?"

"No."

"But your wolf does." Johnny blurted then held his hand up. "Sorry… I shouldn't kiss and tell."

I grumbled, a possessive urge to put my hands on Charlie, claim her as mine, making me take a step forward.

Charlie blushed again, turning toward Johnny. "You remember?"

"Yeah." Johnny rubbed his neck. "Maybe shoulda said something earlier. Didn't want to spook you."

Charlie turned away from him, her gaze lingering on me for a moment, her brow furrowed, before turning back to Levi.

"Yes, in my most recent dreams, I realized that my wolf and I are one. And—" She hesitated, bit her lip in a super sexy way. "When I was running with the pack in the forest, it clicked that I was one with my wolf then, too. I think that's why I was so set on trying the mind-meld thing then. I felt amped up, overconfident. It was foolish." A quick dart of her eyes to me summed up her lingering guilt. "Working together has only ever caused problems for me when my wolf is involved."

I nodded. She wasn't yet forgiven, but I was willing to listen.

"No, I get it. Your wolf side is full of curiosity and very animalistic. That side of you would seek to reform what's been shattered," Levi said in his usual rational way.

"And you think you can help me do the same with my beast?" Her expression softened. "Without a bite?"

"I think we can help you stabilize your beast side. I think she'll recognize what we're doing and work with us," I said. "But you have to let us in...for real."

"All of us, at the same time. You have to take ownership of your mind and call us in like you tried to do with the pack," Levi added, his eyes saying something different to Charlie.

It made me pause long enough to miss the first part of Johnny's words. *She and Levi... There's something more there.*

"...and you have to get rid of the leash and the cage," Johnny said, like it was no big deal.

Piece. Of. Cake.

She shuddered. Shook her head. "I'm not ready."

I wanted to rail against that. She had never been more ready. She needed to step up, take over, be in control of her own power. And yeah, that was coming from my sudden raging urge to dig into what she and Levi had already done together. Obviously they'd been spending time alone while I'd sulked over what she'd done to the pack.

"Those masters hobbled you on purpose," Levi said, echoing my earlier thoughts and pulling me out of my head long enough to get back into the game. "They made you fearful of your own self because they were scared."

"You're able to work with your wolf side, so there's no logical reason why you can't do the same with your beast," Johnny offered. "You just need to stop being so scared."

They were taking the tender approach. Coaxing her with softness. Talking her into it.

"You want me to make friends with my beast self?" Her tone dripped sarcasm. "Why do I feel like I'm stepping into some after school special?"

"We want you to stop being such a damn coward and step up, Charlie." I closed in on her, looming once again. She didn't back away and looked up at me, her eyes hard, lips pulled tight, jaw clenched. "You're weak when you shouldn't be. You're a product of what those outdated, backward masters wanted. It's not what your father wanted for you. It's not what *we* want for you."

"And who are you? My Prince Charming?" It was meant to hurt me, her voice full of razors. "Come to save me from myself?"

I let my lips curl, fangs poking, my intention clear. "I'll do whatever it takes, even if it means saving you from yourself."

Chapter Eight

Charlie

Fangs like Kane's, large and protruding, practically pulsing with the intention to mark me, were only visible like this in his human form when he desired to give a mating bite. It was the only time a male could partially shift.

That was where his mind was right now. That was the skin he had in this game.

It was serious. *He* was serious.

And I was…well, overwhelmed — but not in the way I was expecting.

My body snapped to attention, my core tightened, my nipples hardened. Desire pooled low then high, zinging my brain to act on the impulse, to tilt my head, to give him my throat.

As if I actually wanted him to bite me, to mark me and lay claim.

I swallowed instead, forced those feelings down then squared my shoulders and met his lusty gaze head-on.

"I won't take your bite." I kept my voice steady, even though my whole body wobbled. "You'll have to accept that before I agree to anything."

I expected Kane to flinch, to grit his teeth and clench his fists, but he held my stare then gave one firm nod.

These guys were nuts. And yet...I was intrigued. There was a longing that'd been growing since I first realized these men existed. Not only for them, each in their own way, but a longing to buy what they were selling. I wanted so desperately to have peace within myself, and I thought that was what they were offering. No commitments. No bites. Just helping to fuse what should never have been ripped apart.

I wasn't so stubborn that I couldn't see the truth in their theories. The masters helped me truly discover my werebeast side, coaxed her out to explore her edges, then panicked and shut her down. I never truly had a chance to see what I could do with her on my side.

"We believe in you, Charlie," Levi said. "And we need you."

I flicked my eyes to Levi then Johnny. They seemed so earnest.

I looked at Kane again, his hard eyes narrowed, arms crossed, and I knew he'd never say those words. He'd never submit in the way his brothers would. He wanted me at his side, and he'd sacrifice whatever was necessary to make that happen. Did I believe he'd accept my no-bite stance forever? No. But he would temporarily—and that was acceptable.

For now.

"I'm willing to try." I sighed as if I was reluctantly giving in to their ideas when, really, I was just as eager to see what would happen. I was also scared…terrified. But Kane was right. This was no time to be a coward.

Levi beamed, and he clapped his hands together. "Okay, let's get started." He brushed his hair back from his forehead, clearing his eyes so his view was unobstructed, then he positioned himself in front of me.

"You might want to take a few steps back." I braced myself for whatever they were going to do to get my beast to come out to play. She didn't listen to me when I asked her nicely. It was rage and life-threatening fear that provoked her to make an appearance—the times when she knew I had little control.

Kane moved in behind me, ignoring what I'd just told Levi, and pressed his lips so close to my ear that his breath moved the wisps of stray hair against my cheek. "Sal killed your mother, and you've let him gloat over it for too long."

Instant anger licked up my spine. "What the fu—?"

He swooped down and took me out at the knees, punching the back of my legs so quickly that I hit the ground before I realized what was happening. The fall was awkward, and I hit hard, my full weight landing on my side.

My beast stirred, fists clenched around the bars of my creation, rattling to get out. Her teeth bared. Her eyes locked on Kane.

I jumped up, braced for another hit, arms wide, legs bent, shoulders hunched. I was fighting her back on instinct, so scared of what she could do if I gave her free rein.

"Don't hold her back, Charlie." Levi was still too close, but his arms were open, like he was waiting for the chance to wrap them around me, cage me in his warmth.

My beast roared, not liking the idea of more cages, no matter how good the intentions.

Johnny came at me next. In his wolf, he was as tall as my elbows. He raced forward, nipping at my legs, then moved away before I could spin on him.

"You've let yourself be at the mercy of the men in your life, Charlie," Kane said, his voice coming from behind.

When I turned, he wasn't there.

My beast roared—dizzy, confused anger growing into unmitigated rage.

Kane struck my gut, knocking the wind out of me, making me bend at the waist as pain shot through my core. *Fuck!*

My beast rammed herself against the bars, demanding freedom. I sucked in deep breaths, trying so hard to let her go, but I was scared of what she'd do. I didn't want anyone to get hurt. It was a push and pull that kept her in her cage, her fury building.

"You have to trust us, Charlie," Levi said, moving even closer. "Let her out."

No. I can't. "She'll destroy everything...everyone." I didn't mean to say those words out loud, but they slipped past my clenched jaw.

My beast snarled. I snarled back. She'd *never* been part of me, *never* one with my goals, my life.

I forced myself to stand, moving past the pain of Kane's punch and faced off with him again.

I took a swing to fake him out then swept my legs to knock him down. His calves were like steel beams, but I used a partial shift to put some extra power into the move. He staggered back with a yell. As I went for another kick to take him down, white-hot pain seared into my thigh.

Johnny's claws ripped a gorge along my flesh. I was so shocked that I dropped to my knees then let out a scream full of fury.

My beast rushed me. She pulled me back and threw herself in front. My body transformed in an instant. Fur, fangs, bulk, my frame distorted as she took up more space than I ever could. Her rage blinded me, so I was in the dark, closed off from her awareness, not knowing what she'd do next other than obliterate everything in her way.

"Charlie," a familiar voice echoed in the darkness. "Charlie, Charrrrrlieeeee."

I turned, spinning on an axis I could only feel, searching for the source of the sound.

Panic clenched at my throat, making it close, my heart thundering in my ears. I was surrounded by shadows, lost to the darkness. I was desperate to see something, to know what was going on outside myself, where my beast was raging. She'd never blocked me out like this before. I'd never felt so helpless.

"Charlie…" The voice sounded distant. "Call us in."

"Levi?" I moved toward him, tangled in the opaque web of my mind.

"Call us in, *now*," Kane roared. "You have to. Do. It."

"I don't know how," I screamed, my voice ripped away from me, swallowed by the darkness. Not during chaos. Not like this.

I was flooded with fear, anger, uncertainty, helplessness, so many emotions battering me, urging me to curl up, to hide away—to close my eyes and accept the destruction that she was doing.

I had no control. I had no idea how to pull her back. This was a bad idea.

Terrible.

People would die.

A flash of light so blinding it was painful opened a window outside myself. I squinted, shielded my eyes and saw...Kane bleeding, his furious expression enough to tell me how the fight was going. Johnny, still in his wolf form, was dancing around her, going in for nips and scratches but favoring his left side. Levi was shouting, desperation in his eyes, along with pain. She was going to kill them. She was going to destroy any possibility for me to have a life...

A life with these men.

Not bonded. Not mated. Not bitten. She didn't get to take away the chance I had to be part of a pack, equal footing, arm in arm. She couldn't take away the chance for revenge. My mother, the females that Sal had cut down, they deserved retribution.

I didn't understand my beast. I didn't know why she was the way she was—why I was the way I was. But I knew I'd had enough.

"Stop!" I roared. Then, on instinct, I reached out and gathered all the inky darkness around me. I tugged and yanked, pulling all the threads close before I threw it out again as a web, just like I did with the pack, tossing wildly, hoping to catch all three males in the threads of my mind.

The battle froze. My werebeast halted her attack. There was silence...but not peace. My werebeast was stunned, unsure of what was happening, but she wasn't in my control, not yet, and her rage burned bright, muted only by the strands of the web that had fallen on her.

It wasn't enough.

"Charlie, we're here." Levi's voice infiltrated my awareness. I could see him in the shadows, moving around me, wisps of a solid form. I tried to turn but found I was rooted in place.

"Picture the threads moving closer, cocooning you, Charlie." He brushed against me, and there was light attached to him rather than dark. It stuck to me, too, pulsing to the beat of my heart.

The shadows sparked with bright colors—reds, yellows, purples shooting off in all directions. One was attached to a shadow Kane and one to Johnny, still in his wolf form, as they stepped out of the darkness.

They circled me, moving closer. My beast tried to tear at the threads attached to her, her bloodlust still pumping wickedly through our body.

"Pull her to you." Levi ran fingers along my cheek as he passed me, infusing me with warmth. "Call her into your embrace. Force her there, if necessary."

I didn't know what he meant. He wanted me to hug my inner beast?

"We'll help." Kane moved in next, running ghostly fingers along my throat. "You have to accept her into you."

Johnny's wolf brushed against my hip, his fur tickling my skin. I met his molten eyes and saw encouragement shining there.

I can do this.

I focused on my beast and reached my hands out, arms spread wide. "Come to me," I said, feeling foolish. From my fingers came more threads, anchoring to her, locking into place.

Her head swiveled, her eyes green, menacing. Murder staring back at me.

"Don't make me force you," I growled.

Ghostly hands landed on my shoulders — Kane, Levi on either side. The brush of Johnny's shadow fur nudged my hip, bolstering me...standing with me.

My beast turned, facing off.

I wouldn't ask her again.

With a firm tug, I drew her toward me now that she was cooperating. When she broke through the shadows, I saw what the others had already seen. She was huge, bulging muscles making her monstrous. Fur covered every appendage, marking her as a beast. Her snout was long, fangs gleaming, eyes sharp, hard, cunning, green and coherent. *My eyes* staring back at me. A mirror image full of humanity.

I stepped forward, my legs shaking. She did the same. For every step I took, so did she. When she was close enough, I reached up, dragging my fingers over her jaw to her fangs. She did the same, moving her gnarled hand along my cheek, my lips. I knew I was finally looking at myself, seeing my beast in all her glory.

I was enthralled.

Her fur was glistening, dark, highlighted by the colored threads encircling her. I ran my palm along her collar, and she in turn did the same. She was powerful. She had pent-up aggression that was undeniable but also a desire to be understood that was so vivid to me that I couldn't understand how I'd never felt it before.

I want to be understood. Accepted.

I stepped closer, slipped my arms around her waist — or tried to, anyway — and she did the same, wrapping me up with a tenderness that was both familiar and foreign at the same time.

Kane, Levi and Johnny moved around us, circling, forever circling, and I knew my web, the threads that bound me to these shadow men, were wrapping around my beast and me, connecting us back together — pulling so tight that there was nowhere to go but within.

I closed my eyes and let myself fall.

Chapter Nine

You were there to catch me. Three pairs of arms. A basket of muscle and sinew to cradle my body.

Smoldering lust came like a torrent. The aggression of my beast coursing through every vein, every nerve, every breath and every drop of my blood.

She was me and I was her, and that meant the primal urges that came with my beast side pulsed with intention.

I inhaled your mingled scents, a mix of clove, forest, game, spice, that tickled my throat and teased my senses.

My eyes adjusted in the swirling shadows, reveling in my enhanced sight now that my beast and I were melded.

You, Johnny, grinned like the wily wolf you were, but behind your smile I saw uncertainty.

You, Levi, brushed tender fingers along my cheek and infused in your touch was concern.

You, Kane, tilted my chin, exposed my throat, gripped my neck, then leaned close and claimed my lips. I knew that your actions weren't hiding anything. You were all about possession.

Desire shot through my body, every erogenous zone on fire.

I shivered then moaned against your lips. You swallowed my noises like you were starved for everything I had.

I was lost to your lips, to the hands that caressed my thigh and coaxed my legs open. To the fingers that toyed with my nipples. To the trail of kisses that wound around my breasts, then down my stomach. To the touch of wet, hot heat against my pussy.

The mouth pressed against my clit, tongue flicking, lips sucking, made me writhe, hips rolling, questing for more pressure.

The hands that held my ass, squeezing almost painfully but holding me up, on display, with legs spread wide, made me feel exposed without vulnerability.

The fingers pinching my nipples, teasing but forceful, only to soothe the burn seconds later, made me moan low and deep, a sound that came from my belly and echoed into the shadows.

You were relentless. I didn't even know who the hands or lips or tongues belonged to. You were all over me, coaxing my body to respond with desperate gasps and shaking limbs.

My gums burned as fangs descended and the urge to bite rested just below the surface. I pushed it back, not wanting a bloodbath just when I'd finally embraced my beast. The sensation of my fangs growing didn't abate. It was a partial shift that came with pounding in my brain, like a heartbeat telling me to bitebitebite. A possessive urgency that was so foreign and so right.

My orgasm built in a rush, sending waves along my skin and through my core so my muscles were tight, flexing, desire coiling.

As your lips moved to my mouth once again and your tongue probed inside, flicking against my fangs, I clasped onto you, a partially turned hand, powerful like steel, gripping the back of your neck.

My climax crested, and I yanked away from your lips, tearing myself free from your intoxicating kiss to see molten silver eyes, full of lust. You glanced at my fangs. I wrenched your head to the side.

And you let me. You let me get close enough to bite.

Surprise knocked me back.

You'd take my bite?

I scraped my fangs along your flesh, and you groaned.

Yes, you'd take my bite.

My body exploded with shockwaves of pleasure. You'd exposed your throat, knowing for sure that I was not going to kiss you. Knowing that I was going to mark you as mine or perhaps rip your throat right out of your body.

My beast and I couldn't possibly be fused.

She wanted blood and craved death. She belonged in a cage for the way she was acting, urging me to wreak havoc.

I'd be damned if I put you in danger of my wild, uncontrollable self, no matter what my instincts demanded.

Chapter Ten

Johnny

Charlie wasn't fusing with her beast side—not completely, anyway. "You think she's resisting on purpose?" I poured myself another whiskey while Kane reset the video. "Holding herself back?" Call it paranoia or just plain insecurity, but part of me thought she was refusing to fully bond with her beast side because she was scared of what it could mean for us.

She liked us. She desired us. She wanted to be part of the pack. She was holding herself back. I didn't blame her after what she'd gone through.

"I think on a subconscious level she's terrified of being hurt again, but I don't think that's the problem." Kane hit play and we watched as he took Charlie through a series of drills meant to retrain her reflexes to incorporate her beast side into her battle techniques without losing her shit completely. They'd been at it relentlessly for days, and each session ended with

Charlie beasting out with some level of control, only to lose her grip on herself and end up needing to be subdued.

"See? Right there." Kane pointed to the screen. We've got the training video playing on his fifty-inch mounted monitor, blowing up every nuance in the fight. "She pulls her punch here."

We watched as she stepped back from an obvious opening where she could have put Kane on his ass — and then some.

"She's battling with her beast side still like it's a separate entity. She might have started some kind of bonding process with her inner beast, but she hasn't accepted that side of herself completely, and I think it's because she's scared that she'll hurt us." Kane had an unreadable expression on his face, but I'd like to think he appreciated the subtle loyalty she was showing us. Maybe he'd soften his bark toward her and stop being so difficult when we suggested he spend some down time with her.

Kane said he was pushing her for her own good and for our mutually beneficial goals. We wanted justice on Sal just as much as Charlie did.

"She's wasting time."

As much as I wanted to let my heart melt over her consideration for our safety, Kane was right. We needed her on her game and melded with her beast side if we were going to move her forward.

"What do you suggest we do?" I swirled my drink, taking in the smoky oak scent, my mouth watering for the first taste.

As I raised my glass to my lips, Kane tore his eyes away from the monitor to look at me, his expression grim. "I think it's time for the real deal."

"Pay a visit to her uncle?" I slammed the drink, reveling in the searing heat of expensive whiskey pounding down my throat. I wanted to savor it, but this revelation was a big deal from Kane. "Thank fuck! It's about time." I'd been itching to go after that asshole since Levi dug up what had truly happened to Charlie while she'd been training her uncle's ferals three years ago.

"Gareth is her uncle on her mother's side," Kane reminded me. "So, he doesn't have the same clout as Sal Larsen."

"Still an alpha to be wary of." Levi slid into the conversation like he'd been here the whole time. "He's got an army of highly trained wolves."

"That he pays for loyalty." I put my glass down. "They're more like mercenaries rather than a clan."

"Yeah, but he pays well, from what I've heard, and they've taken his bite, so they're committed." Kane called up a live aerial feed to display on the screen. "He's at his summer house this month."

"He has a handful of wolves with him." Levi pointed to the scattering of guards on site. "Not his full pack."

"Confident, isn't he?" I scanned the grounds, curious as to how we suddenly had an aerial view of Gareth's place. His cabin was nestled into the Rockies, built right into the side of a mountain. It might have looked cozy and relaxed with a clearing in the forest, next to a spring-fed pond but I could tell that it wasn't chosen just for its idyllic views. "Even if the cabin has one way in." I pointed to the access road leading to the house. "He must think he's untouchable to have so few wolves with him."

"He rotates them." Levi pointed to the screen. "And he's got a hell of a security system in place. It took me forever to hack into this drone feed."

I should have known—my brother, the geek of all things.

"Of course, you infiltrated his security."

"I called in a favor, helped me bypass some of Gareth's protections." Levi nodded to the screen. "We should let Charlie have her day with her uncle. Let him see what she can do."

"Because the training is going so well?" Kane rubbed the back of his neck. "She's not ready."

"She's resisting embracing her beast because she has no stakes yet," Levi said, a contradiction to what Kane was saying earlier about her not wanting to hurt us, but still, a valid point. Maybe those two reasons weren't exclusive, either. Charlie was a complex woman with many different, competing desires, motivations, goals.

It was possible that the fight wasn't real enough for her yet. Sure, she was angry, and she wanted a piece of her stepbrother, but she wasn't pushing for action. Fear, my gut said, was holding her back—fear for us, fear for herself, fear of what her beast could do.

"We need to get her in the action," Levi continued. "Up the stakes so she has a taste of long-overdue revenge." He waved his hand. "She's been hiding for too long."

"A trial run?" I liked it. "When do we leave?"

"Hang on..." Kane cued the video of their latest training session where Charlie lost her shit about five minutes into the fight. "We can't just whet her appetite and think there won't be risks."

"We're not going in blind, and her beast side is exactly what Gareth and his goons need to experience," Levi said, his arms folded. "We'll make sure the team who goes with her will know when to get out of her way." When Kane started to argue, Levi cut him off.

"We need to show her what she can do with the right motivation. Her uncle has it coming."

Kane studied the video again, frozen on Charlie's transformed face, her eyes blazing, fangs bared and muzzle scrunched mid-roar. She was a force.

"We can't stop her once she goes beast like this." Kane sighed. "We can't show any weakness in front of another pack."

"No, we let her go. We let her do her thing." I couldn't help grinning. I was amped up and ready for a fight.

"And if she gets caught up in bloodlust?" Kane turned to face us. "We can't all go with her."

"Like I said, we make sure our guys are fully prepped," Levi said.

"I'm going with her," I said, cracking my knuckles. "I'll be her wingman. She listens to me when I step into her world."

"Johnny does seem to have a calming effect on her beast."

"Your attention will be divided," Kane said, his tone more resigned than enthusiastic. "You won't be able to fight if you're in her head, too."

He was speaking from experience. We hadn't quite mastered how to project ourselves into her mind and stay with it enough to protect ourselves out in the real world.

"Don't worry about me." I had faith in Charlie. "I'll make sure things stay cool."

Kane shot a look at Levi, who shrugged in response. "You know how I feel about this."

"Okay, fine. We move forward. Johnny, go collect a team and brief them." He nodded my way. "And make sure Lex and Ari are with you."

I gave him a salute and turned toward the door.

"I'll update Charlie," Levi said as he followed me.

"No," Kane barked. "I will. She needs to hear this as a command rather than a rousing pep talk."

I shared a look with Levi, who had his mouth open to presumably argue, but Kane was already out of the door.

"Kane is flame to her accelerant," I said as a way of an explanation we both didn't really need. "Maybe he'll rile her up the right way."

"Yeah, 'cause that's been working out for him just great during training." Levi rolled his eyes.

It wasn't uncommon for us to poke at each other, criticize the way brothers do, but Levi's sarcasm hit differently.

"What the alpha wants..." I shrugged, trying to redirect.

"I just hope he's ready to step down when it's time for her to step up," Levi mumbled as he pushed past me. It was the first time in a long time that I'd heard him doubt Kane's leadership. It was the first time in my life I'd heard him do it behind Kane's back.

By the time I stepped out of the den, Levi was gone, so there was no opportunity to dig into his statement. It made me wonder, though, if our brotherhood was strong enough to withstand the Charlie selection process. As time went on and she didn't choose one of us—never mind all of us—to mark her, the bigger the rift between us would grow.

We each wanted her, and she continued to call us into her dreams, so the feeling was mutual, at least when she had her guard down. I understood her hesitation to take on a harem of wolves, brothers on top of that, but she had been the first to call us in and now our innate competitiveness was rearing as it became clear that she was stalling, unsure what to do.

Was the harem idea off the table? No idea. If it was and she was in the process of determining which of us she wanted as a mate, then things were going to get ugly.

Charlie needed to decide...soon, or we wouldn't make it to the grand finale and take down Sal. We'd be too busy taking down each other.

Chapter Eleven

Charlie

I wasn't expecting Kane to be on the other side of my bedroom door when I swung it open. His knock wasn't what I'd expect from a hulking control freak like him. It was tentative, soft...respectful.

"Oh...it's you."

Kane had his hands clasped in front of him and his head bowed.

When he looked up at me, his eyes radiated heat, like moving lava that seared me straight to the gut. "We need to talk."

"You...talk?" I shrugged, trying for cool when he gave me a raised eyebrow. "I thought you only barked orders."

There was a lump in my stomach that made me instantly nauseated. What the fuck did he want to talk about now? Was he kicking me out? Had he decided that this was all a waste of his time?

It wasn't like I'd been completely successful with adapting to his training and melding to my beast had been difficult. She was still in a cage most of the time. I was too scared to give her free rein, even if I could now tap into her mind and understand her motivations. Her desires were full of rage and chaos, and rationalizing with her only worked in fragments. I couldn't accept her need to bite any of these men. Not even Kane deserved her ferocity.

He narrowed his eyes and thinned his lips, and it made me wonder if he did, in fact, come here to bark some orders.

"Well, come in then. Let's talk." I gestured to my room, which was way too big for one person. It was a suite, complete with a private bathroom, jacuzzi tub included, a bigger-than-king-sized bed that I could starfish on and still not reach the edges and a sitting area with a double-wide plush couch that I'd sunk into after many sparring sessions. There were other amenities that made this place hard to even think about leaving, like the impossibly high thread count and laundry service. In all, the entire place was twice the size of my whole apartment in Toronto but a lot less homely.

Kane didn't sit on one of two loungers in the seating area. Instead, he leaned against the back of one, forgetting—or maybe not knowing—that they were rockers. I stifled a laugh when the forward sway caught him off guard and he stumbled a step.

So not graceful. Made me wonder if he was nervous.

I frowned. Why would Mr. King Alpha be nervous talking to me?

The rock in my gut grew twice as big, and I was tempted to run to the bathroom to puke or at least lock myself in there so I didn't have to hear what he'd come to say.

"What's up?" My voice sounded strangled, despite my forced calm.

He didn't seem to notice.

He'd left the chair and was looking out of the window, something I'd noticed he liked to do when he had hard news to share.

"We think it's time for you to meet with your uncle."

His back was to me, so he didn't see how hard I flinched or how my hand fluttered to my throat. Flashes of blood and gore, violence and rage rushed through my mind, tapping every fear I'd ever had where my beast was concerned. I hadn't faced my uncle since his men had brought my beast to her knees after killing the pack of ferals around me. His soldiers had been a fraction of a second away from decapitating me — or, at least, were ready to try. My uncle had been screaming for me to shift back to myself. I'd managed, somehow, to pull myself out of her rage and force her back into her cage so I could be present again. I think that's the only thing that saved my life that day. The look of horror on my uncle's face at seeing my transformation was enough to scar me alone, but knowing that all around me were the remains of my fellow wolves left a wound that had never healed.

"I can't go back there." It slipped out, and I hated how weak I sounded. "I don't know what my beast will do."

Even now, with just the mention of my uncle, my beast rattled the cage, clawing to get out, eager for justice, revenge, blood.

Kane's shoulders hunched. I knew he hated it when I referred to my beast as a separate entity. No matter how many times we tried to use the mental threads to connect me and her, there was still something missing. I hated going into her psyche…my psyche, that part of me who was an unhinged beast.

Even though they said otherwise, the men *all* thought what I needed was a bite from them. I knew Levi was convinced that the drawings he'd studied depicted that level of connection, a bonding bite, to really have an impact. Even if what he told me was different, I knew, deep down, that's what he ultimately wanted. I knew Johnny thought it would only strengthen us all if we committed with a bite. Kane? He was after possession and made no excuses about it.

I chose to resist their theories. I might have been cool with submissive games in dreamland or, one day maybe, in my bedroom, but I wasn't so easily swayed with that kind of submission in real life.

"You're going on a mission with Johnny…to your uncle's. I've already made arrangements. You'll maintain control over your beast side," Kane said, his voice firm, like he was giving a command. I might have believed that it was the only way he knew how to speak, but I'd heard him when he was tender, after we'd played and fucked and satiated one another in my dreams.

"Your uncle may hold information about Andrew's whereabouts." To him this was non-negotiable duty. I *would* go to find out what my uncle knew, because it was what Kane wanted me to do.

"I don't see how. He and Andrew were never close." I was grasping at straws because I really didn't know what kind of relationship Andy and my uncle Gareth had had in the last three years.

Kane shot a hard look over his shoulder. "You know your uncle was planning on bidding on you, too, right?"

His words floored me. *No. No. Not again.* I stumbled back, banging up against the side of the couch. My knees gave way, and I slumped down on the arm rest.

Leave it to Kane, landing a sucker-punch to get his point across.

"He was planning on taking you for himself, finishing what he started three years ago at his compound...bypassing consent." Kane turned to me, and I watched warily as he moved closer. "Men like him will not be denied... Men like him have something to prove." Kane cracked his knuckles. "I'd say it's time for a chat with the man. Let him know what you think of his behavior."

I knew he was trying to rile me up, to get my blood pumping, wanting revenge, but I was exhausted — not physically, but emotionally. I couldn't go back there. I couldn't face the memories. The ghost of bloodshed would be everywhere. It would be a fist to the heart all over again.

I couldn't go back there because my beast was spiraling, even as we spoke, and I knew I'd lose control. I knew there would be blood on my hands once again.

"I can't go after every man who has wronged me."

Kane's eyes flashed a rusty red. "Why not?" He yanked me up by the arm and gave me a shake that rattled my brain enough to piss me off. "You're telling me that you'd rather hide in a hole and pretend that these men don't deserve your wrath?"

"What's the point?" I tried to shrug but his grip tightened. "It's not like bringing down my uncle will do anything. Men like him are everywhere."

"What's the point?" Kane barked. "Are you for real?" He glared, and I could practically see sparks flying. "You're meant to be all powerful, Charlotte. You are meant to be the — "

"Savior of all female wolves… Yeah, yeah…" I tried to tug my arm away but he wasn't letting go. "It's a fantasy. *Your* fantasy. I can't do it."

"Wha — ?"

"I can't even keep my beast under control!" I yelled then pushed him back using a partial shift to get his brick-house body to move an inch. "It'll start a war!"

He released my arm but leaned into me, so close that spit hit my face. "So let her loose. Stop being so fucking terrified. Start. A. War."

Floored by his words, my mouth opened, then closed, no sounds tumbling out. He held my stare, unflinching.

"It's the men who have wronged you who should be feeling fear."

"So, *what*? You want me to stroll over to my uncle's place and give him a piece of my mind?" I waved my arms around chaotically, scrambling to follow his logic. "Then if my beast decides she wants a taste, which she will because I'll be freaking the fuck out, I'm just supposed to let her go?"

Kane pulled back enough for me to take in his expression. His eyes were alive, heat pouring out of him. His lips curled. I almost expected to see his fangs poking out.

"Oh fuck, that's exactly what you think should happen."

I shook my head then started to pull away, but he clasped his hand around the back of my neck and pulled me into him again. His heat enveloped me. His scent, musky clove and sea salt, snaked up my nose and made my mouth water. His eyes hooded, the amber glow pulsing past his dark lashes. I looked at his lips, so close, so firm.

I wanted to tilt my head and let him take me. I wanted him to make the first move. I wanted him to do what we both needed, what we'd both been dancing around for days.

"You must stop holding back," he growled, his voice a tumble of gravel.

I rested my arm along his hip, my fingers splayed against his lower back. "I could say the same thing to you."

He flinched, and something dark flashed over his face. Desire pooled in my gut. My breasts ached, crushed up against his chest. I wanted to rock against him. I wanted to taste him.

He squeezed the back of my neck then yanked my head to the side, his other hand in my hair, tangled and tugging. "You don't want this."

I licked my lips in response. *Of course I do.*

He gulped. Tried to glare me into changing my mind. Then he gave in and slammed his lips against mine—hard, punishing, taking what he wanted. He waited for less than a heartbeat before forcing his tongue past my lips and devouring me whole.

* * * *

I wasn't saying Kane's kiss changed my mind about going to face my uncle, but his kiss did shoot me straight into the stratosphere, so when Johnny came to collect me for our mission, I was floating so high I couldn't form words to argue.

Was that Kane's tactic? Kiss me into oblivion so I'd comply?

After he'd ravaged me for a good eternity of minutes with his long, breath-stopping, tongue-sucking kiss, he pulled back, ran a hand through his hair then beelined out of my room like he'd touched a forbidden totem and couldn't cope. I was too stunned to actually do anything about it, floating outside of myself.

Kane kissed me.

He'd kissed me, and it wasn't punishment. It wasn't delayed gratification. He gave in and kissed me — and he loved it. He loved it so much that it had scared him out of my room.

After Kane had run, I'd slumped onto the couch in a daze, still there when Johnny had poked his head in my door and asked if I knew the plan.

My slight nod was all he needed to get me up and hustling with him to the waiting car.

And that was where I found myself, not on my way to my uncle's compound but headed to his vacation house in the mountains. As if that made it less of a problem. It was still a place that triggered me all the same. I'd been to Uncle Gareth's cottage many times throughout my childhood, always with my mom and sometimes with my stepbrothers.

My mom… Gareth's most beloved sister.

A pang of loss rocked me, taking me by surprise. I'd mourned my mother deeply, heavily, when I had been a child, and the thought of dredging up memories of better days, fun times at my uncle's vacation home, sat like a boulder on my heart. Another reason not to go.

But the ghost of Kane's kiss still burned on my lips, and I kept touching myself there as if to prove that it had actually happened in real life. He wanted me to go face Gareth. He wanted me to let my beast have her way. All I could think about was how I'd finally broken

Kane out of his armor. I didn't know what the hell that meant, other than that my heart was all drippy and soft and I wanted more of what he'd given me. I wanted to make him proud.

Mix that in with the turmoil of the past and memories of my mother, and I wasn't at all the right frame of mind for heading into potential battle.

"Your uncle is expecting us," Johnny said as he tapped on his phone. "Kane reached out."

"Wonderful." There was no turning back now. "Great plan. Now he has time to gather his posse of elite killers."

"He doesn't think this is an ambush." Johnny grinned. He was beaming like a kid on the way to a theme park. "Even though it is."

The rest of the envoy were traveling in an SUV behind us, a whole half dozen of highly skilled weres — the correct amount of back up for whatever was about to go down, according to Johnny. He felt it would be more appropriate to arrive as emissaries in appearance, which was why we were turning onto the service road that led to my uncle's place in Johnny's Maserati. He swore as he tried to maneuver around the potholes, and I swear he'd cry buckets if any of the branches leaned down to scratch his cherry-red baby.

"Kane said we're after information. What is it you expect me to do?"

Johnny cocked an eyebrow my way, compelling me to continue.

"Kane wants me to let loose and get what I'm owed." *A reckoning.* "I doubt my beast will be much for talking once she gets going."

"You focus on doing what you need to do to square up with your uncle." Johnny tapped his head. "I'm interested in seeing how things play out organically." He cursed as the car dipped into another divot in the road. "You'd think with all this guy's money, he'd do something about this road."

I turned away from him to look out of the window. The trees that I used to race through were larger, fuller but also familiar in the way they zigzagged. I used to love shifting then exploring through my uncle's property as a wolf — taking in all the smells, hunting the small game, enjoying the little freedom I was afforded in the safety of my uncle's land. Little did I know what was coming for me after I went through puberty. Once it became clear to those around me that my father had no intention of trading me into the service of one of his pals or relatives, my uncle had become furious.

The boulder in my gut was back with a vengeance. My uncle took great offense to being denied a chance to mate with me — his niece. Before my mother had died...*was murdered*, I reminded myself — she had warned me of her brother's fury over my father's insistence that I was unavailable and off the roster for mating. Even though I was only a child and puberty was miles away, as far as I was concerned, I didn't believe her and neither did my dad — not until years later, after she was long dead and buried and my uncle had attempted to trap me with the intention of forcing a bond. He'd assaulted me, incited my darker side, which then led to a rising up of the army of ferals who I'd unwittingly made loyal to me.

Rage simmered at the memory of their sacrifice for me. "If my beast gets her way, there won't be anyone left to interrogate." I closed my eyes, tamped down the memories that caused so much pain and fury, then tried to tap into her mind while things were calm, before my anger got the better of me.

Don't fuck this up.

She swiveled her enormous head my way, narrowed her eyes and curled one side of her furry lip, baring teeth that I swear were already streaked in blood.

I took that to be a firm 'fuck you', werebeast style.

Chapter Twelve

Charlie

"My darling niece!" Uncle Gareth came out of his cottage, which looked like a cliché old-timey homestead with its huge log walls and bark shingles, complete with a porch and rocker. He had his arms wide with a familiar smarmy smile in place and looked the same as he had three years ago, a gigolo in his too-tight gun-metal-gray pants and his chest-baring paisley button-up. He lifted his aviator sunglasses to scoop his salt-and-pepper hair, which gave him an eighties vibe. "It's so wonderful to see you."

I froze on the spot, unable to move a step closer and put myself in range of his arms. A nod was the best I could do as I crossed my arms, narrowed my eyes and send a clear back-the-fuck-off message. "Uncle."

"Alpha Gareth, thank you for welcoming us." Johnny offered his hand, and I knew it was a deflection for my cool greeting.

My uncle sneered briefly at me, there and gone in a flash, as he took Johnny's hand. "I see she hasn't changed in her time away." He shook Johnny's hand briskly. "Still headstrong."

"Thank you for agreeing to meet." Johnny deflected again. "As Kane mentioned, we're here to talk."

"Yes, well, had I known there would be lingering hard feelings, I'd have suggested you keep the female at home. These women can hold a grudge, am I right?" He winked and laughed like I wasn't standing right here ready to rip his motherfuc—*calm down...stay in control.*

My beast surged forward, threatening to yank me out of the way so she could come out to play.

Instead of reacting, I made sure my expression stayed neutral. I uncrossed my arms, let my hands brush against my thighs, took a deep, quiet breath then did what Levi and I had been practicing for days. I tapped into my beast's essence, easing myself alongside her, melding in my own way with her emotions, her rolling rage, recognizing for the millionth time that what she felt was what I felt, just a thousand degrees more intense.

She's you. You're her. Now get your shit together.

"I suppose congratulations are in order." Gareth turned his back to me, letting me know that I didn't exist, that I wasn't a threat, that he wasn't scared of me.

When really, we all knew, he was.

"You've finally done what my brother-in-law bragged would only happen over his dead body." He threw a pointed look over his shoulder at me. "Claimed his precious daughter."

I gritted my teeth, seething. My beast shook her giant head, knocking me loose from her essence so I was suddenly on the outside looking at her spit flying, teeth gnashing, eyes blazing fury. I clawed my way back into her consciousness, forcing myself to awareness, embracing her anger but tempering it.

Not yet. Hold steady. Be smart.

I took a step toward him, my fists clenched, along with my jaw, breathing slow, even though my heart was thundering and flames of rage licked at my nerves, making me shake.

"Oh, you're mistaken there." Johnny pierced me with a beseeching expression that could be a call to action or a plea for calm. Either way, his eyes danced, and his lips curled and I knew, no matter what happened, he'd have my back. "She hasn't been claimed. She's been positioned."

"Positioned?" My uncle shifted to glance at me, his face screwed up.

"On the gameboard."

I sensed the rest of our team stepping up behind me and Johnny and it felt just like it did when my loyal ferals had done the same thing three years ago, facing off with my uncle once again. I was empowered. I was in control.

My beast accepted the situation and eased back, allowing me to rule the tide of emotions for now.

"She wants to play with the big boys, does she?" My uncle scanned the group of men then glanced at me with a sweeping look, before turning his gaze back to Johnny. "I suppose she comes by it honestly. Her father was a real feminist with her, raised her to think she was on equal footing." He scoffed like he was talking to a likeminded werewolf. "I respect Kane's move to place her in the action. She is a powerful beast. I know her to be an asset in many ways." He didn't look at me when he said, "If you can tame her, that is."

A growl slipped past my lips.

"Those sound like fighting words, Gareth," Johnny said with a smile. He shook his head, and again I didn't know if he was sending a message for me to cool it or amp it up. "We aren't here for trouble."

Lies.

"We're here to talk."

"Kane said you're here to settle a misunderstanding." My uncle's eyes gleamed, a sneer warping his face. "I take that to mean he wants to form an alliance. With Sal in the game, things have gotten... testy."

"We are here to settle." 'A score' went unsaid. Johnny had a calm expression, unreadable to anyone who didn't know better. I saw quiet cunning, a play on words, the intention to strike when least expected. *Not yet though. Not yet.* "We're looking for Andrew Larsen. Hoping you might have some intel on his whereabouts."

Gareth frowned. "Why would I have any information about that SOB?" He waved his hand. "You're wasting your time if you're here for information on Andrew."

Johnny folded his arms and leaned back a little. "We've heard you might have helped him get out of Vancouver."

I was startled to learn that tidbit and narrowed my eyes, first on Johnny, then quickly back on my uncle. Why didn't I know about this before now? Why was I out of the loop when it came to clan information?

Because you won't commit. No secret there, genius.

"Oh, is that what you heard?" Gareth squinted, pursed his lips, rolled his tongue along the inside of his cheek so it bulged out.

It's true. Oh fuck. He's involved.

I took a step back. My beast reared. I flexed my fingers, clenched and unclenched my jaw, grinding my molars as they started to grow bigger. I fought to keep myself from slipping control by using the techniques I'd been practicing to stay grounded with my beast.

Breathe in. Breathe out. Ride the wave of rage. Let it peak. Tamp it down. Start again.

"Where's Andrew?" I kept my voice steady but stern, doing my best to stay as cool as Johnny while my beast continued to rage on the inside. "You know."

Gareth tilted his head, scrutinizing me like I was a disobedient dog. It was an expression, I'd learned, that all male weres gave, one they honed from birth, it seemed. I wanted to smack it off his face.

"You're losing your grip again, aren't you, niece?" He motioned behind him, so his men began to close in. "You haven't gotten that beast of yours under control, have you?" He looked at Johnny. "Are you aware of my niece's...deformity?"

It was a slap that shouldn't have stung as much as it did. My beast roared within and my body spasmed, muscles stretching, building, bulking, fangs poking into my gums, burning as they dropped. I took deep breaths, tried to rein things in. I didn't want a bloodbath, no matter how much I loathed the man.

The beast and I were one. I reminded myself. A swirling mantra that pounded through my mind. *We are one...we are one...we are—*

"Don't insult my intelligence, Gareth." Johnny sighed as he briefly rubbed his thumb and finger on the bridge of his nose. He was so good at making you think you were wasting his time. "You set Andrew up on the flight and offered some contacts in Toronto," Johnny continued. "We just need to know where he is now. We have some questions for him."

"Have you tricked these men into thinking you're stable, Charlotte?" My uncle ignored Johnny as he turned toward me. "Do they know what a freak you are?"

I stood my ground, continued with the deep breaths, but my body was bigger than it should be, taking on a partial shift on the way to full beast mode.

"You're just like your mother," he said with a sneer, moving closer when he should've been turning back. "Never knew her place, either. That fool of a man, Dominic, always gave too far-reaching freedom to her and you." He lifted his finger, stabbing the air, his lips curled and eyes fierce. "She had a mouth on her, too, your mother. Headstrong. Stubborn. Entitled." He spit the last word as he scorched me with another up and down, taking in my growing size, my monstrous deformities. "If you ask me, your mother deserved what she got in the end."

The air left my body. My heart stopped. Red flashed across my vision. *He knew.* Until this moment, I didn't really believe... I mean...Kane had said...but I didn't really think that she was murdered by her own stepson, that my father had no idea. But my uncle knew. Her own brother knew. She was murdered and these puny men, werewolves so used to power and control, obviously felt she'd deserved it.

I'd had enough of this testosterone-riddled world.

"You...*bastard*," I roared, then let my beast go.

Chapter Thirteen

Levi

"Well, that didn't take long," I said as I zoomed in on the action.

Kane leaned closer to the screen as well, his jaw tight, eyes blazing.

Charlie shifted to beast mode in two seconds flat.

"Keep the camera on her," Kane said. "I want to make sure this isn't a setup."

"Don't worry, Kane." I adjusted the drone to take a wide view and captured the battle as it rolled out. "Gareth didn't see this coming." The guy truly thought his niece was visiting to grovel. "I tapped into his phone. Gareth is so old school that he has a landline." I shook my head and chuckled. "Caught a conversation with his head of security. Downplayed the danger of Charlie coming." Not to mention completely misreading Johnny as the playboy sidekick to Kane and dismissed me outright as a non-issue. "His ego is so huge, he actually planned to humiliate her without repercussions."

Kane snorted, but his eyes were steady on the chaos as it unfolded. I knew he'd rather be there, in the heat of things with Charlie, but she needed to test her boundaries without us looming. Johnny was the best choice to escort her to this fight because he hadn't been working as closely with her to retrain her mind. He wasn't tangled up in her inner conflict as much as Kane and I were.

I typed a few commands, intercepting a call for backup from Gareth's security on site. There wouldn't be anyone coming to the rescue. Gareth was going to have to face his demons today.

Charlie was imposing in full beast mode, but she was also smooth and skilled as she took on the wolves who had come to protect her uncle. She swiped and kicked, using claws and the threat of fangs to take them out, one by one, knocking them down, over and over until they didn't get up again.

"She's not killing them." Kane sounded in awe, and I didn't blame him. This was the first time Charlie had been in her beast form and hadn't completely succumb to bloodlust. "She's taking them down, but she's not delivering a killing blow."

"She has more control than she thinks she does," I said, equally as in awe but also near giddy with the proof that I'd been right all along. She was the alpha queen. She was keeping them alive because she knew they'd bow to her in time.

The fight continued with Johnny and his team setting Gareth's wolves up, putting them in Charlie's path so she could knock them down. Blood was flying.

Fur floated in the air. Gareth had run toward the cottage as if that would save him.

Charlie's head came up, swiveled in her uncle's direction, then she leapt and, in a beautiful takedown, she landed on his back and forced him to the ground.

She heaved him over so her snout was in his face. "You will submit," she growled.

"Did you hear that?" Even I was surprised. She'd never been able to speak coherently while in beast form. I looked at Kane, whose eyes were wide, shock plain on his face.

Charlie wrapped her clawed hands around Gareth's throat, blood spurted from flesh wounds, not enough to suggest she was puncturing veins or arteries but enough to show her intent. "Where is Andrew?"

Gareth may have been full of ego, but he wasn't stupid. He knew what Charlie was capable of.

"H-h-he f-failed his m-mission," Gareth sputtered.

"What mission?"

"To capture you."

Charlie settled back, crushing Gareth's legs with her weight. He screamed. She sneered.

"You sent him." It wasn't a question.

Gareth murmured something unintelligible.

"Why?"

"To put you in your place." He gasped as Charlie tightened her grip. "To put a leash on you, like your father should have when you were born."

"My *place*," she roared as she leaned in again, her fangs gleaming.

Gareth shuddered, a look of pure revulsion on his face. Charlie lifted her head and roared into the sky, spit flying, fangs gleaming.

Kane leaned closer to the screen. Every muscle in my body was tense.

Charlie lowered her head slowly.

"My place, Uncle, is right here."

She lunged quickly then bit, sinking her fangs deep into the dip between Gareth's shoulder and throat.

Ohhhhh fuck.

Kane pushed himself away from the desk like he was ready to bolt out of here.

"Wait...Kane..."

Gareth's scream died as Charlie ripped her mouth away, blood flying.

The wound healed instantly.

"What the—?"

"Look." Kane pointed as he settled down again. "Zoom in."

I did as he said and watched as a web-like bruise spread with tendrils that slipped under Gareth's shirt.

He contorted violently. His men stayed down. Biding their time? Or something else?

Charlie jumped off Gareth, her mouth gaping, fangs dripping with blood.

Johnny motioned for our pack members to stand down. Everyone watched, waiting, unsure what would happen next.

Gareth's body shook, his chest arched out, his jaw clenched.

"Is he shifting?"

"Trying to," Kane said.

Charlie took another step back, like she wanted to run. Her chest heaved. She let out a shuddering breath.

Gareth rolled himself to all fours, panting, clearly in pain. He didn't lift his head but turned, moving slowly on hands and knees until he reached Charlie's feet.

"My queen," he said, then lowered himself so his forehead touched the ground.

His men all did the same, dropping to their knees, murmuring the formal address as if she'd just become their leader.

Because she *had* just become their alpha.

Charlie looked up, her eyes wide, disbelief, maybe even fear, warring, but before her beast side could go ballistic, she shuddered, her fur vibrating, skin rolling then shifted back to her human form. She took a moment to compose herself then turned to Johnny with an expression of barely contained shock.

"Get me out of here."

Chapter Fourteen

Charlie

What the fuck just happened?

Threads had been formed. I was connected to Gareth in ways I'd never wanted to be. I was bound to his men, all of them — even the ones who weren't present at his cottage.

Sounds echoed in my skull, teasing my ears, a buzz that would torment in time.

They were in my head, Gareth and his pack, dozens of them. Their voices were murmuring like whispers from nowhere. I felt them and, when I closed my eyes, I saw threads of my web alight and vibrating. One thing about werewolves was that they knew power when they felt it. They had all bowed on bended knee to me.

I'd taken over his pack.

Oh my fucking —

I clenched my head, fingers gripping my hair and winced. They were going to drive me insane. The constant chatter was practically deafening. They sought answers. They wanted direction.

Alpha, they pleaded, *what do we do?*

They were talking to me, I realized. My beast growled, not liking the intrusion. *Be still.* I ordered, intending for her to stay calm.

The volume lowered to nothing. I frowned. *Did I do that?* I turned inward, searching for an explanation. As I sought the voices of Gareth's pack, they returned, a jumbled mess of noise.

Quiet.

My beast settled as sudden silence brought peace.

Every muscle, every joint, every nerve ending in my body unclenched.

What the fuck is happening?

It wasn't that the quiet brought only peace. It brought a rightness that was foreign to me but that I'd craved my whole life—a thing I'd never been able to explain or understand, a hole that had needed filling. My bones, my blood, my brain all resonated with acceptance. *They're mine now.* This was how it was meant to be.

My beast side was satiated for the first time in my life. She was calm. I was *in* control and not fighting *for* control of my mind. I didn't sense her pent-up rage and aggression.

What I felt was satisfaction.

What I felt was confidence.

What I felt was power.

And now Gareth's pack felt it, too.

"What happened there?" Johnny asked. He was tentative, seemingly unsure.

I hated that I was making him worry.

"I don't know."

What I did know was that a bite from a shifted werewolf infected a target, turning them from human to werewolf at the first full moon — *if* they survived the transformation. Each night leading up to the full moon would bring degrees of agony as their body slowly morphed from human to beast. Their unnecessary human parts died, decaying, while they were still alive and aware. The necessary ones changed, bulked up, transformed. It was torture. Many didn't live to see the full moon. Those who did were sometimes so traumatized that they were feral beyond repair and needed to be put down immediately.

It was only the males who could bite like that. Or, at least, it had only ever been the males who had created ferals, who had created packs. The bite tied the new wolf to the one who bit them. It didn't force loyalty, but it made it hard for the new werewolf to turn on their creator. Or, at least, that was the way our mythology went. The stronger the werewolf who bit, the stronger the connection, the stronger the pack.

I was beginning to think that everything I thought I knew about werewolf lore was wrong.

"*My queen.*"

I shuddered as my uncle's words rolled on a loop through my head. I wanted to scrub it from my memories. Forget it ever happened.

What have I done?

In born-werewolf families, the blood ties bonded each of us to one another, but blood didn't mean loyalty. Born-werewolves were rare and therefore had an elevated position in our society. Loyalty came through social constructs of respectability, through wealth and most effectively through fear. No werewolf wanted to be ousted from their family clan, which meant most werewolves stayed in line.

To bite a born wolf like my uncle… To bite a family member… It was definitely stepping out of bounds. It was unheard of.

It's taboo.

I'd crossed lines that no one would dare cross. Not only did I bite but I did it to a werewolf and an alpha. I should have been horrified. I should have been scared for my life. Instead, I felt empowered. Gareth had bowed to me. His men were mine, with loyalty that felt unquestionable.

That made me…

Alpha. A guttural version of my inner voice rattled me to reality. *You're alpha now.*

Even though my beast took the bite, I'd condoned it. I was there, with her, doing what felt natural.

Primal instinct.

My mind returned to Levi's photos, the scrolls and depictions of female beasts in their glory. The markings on the wolves by her side were starbursts, not webs — a different kind of mark.

If I were to bite another wolf while I was in human form, like partially shift only my fangs just like the males did with a mating bite, what would I produce? What would come of that?

I felt like I already knew the answer, but I was not, in any way, ready to test it.

I'd bitten my uncle in my beast form, and I'd created a link that made him subservient. If I bit another werewolf in my human form…would I create a bond, an unbreakable bond?

"Charlie." Johnny's voice was hesitant.

"I turned my uncle," I said, my eyes still on the trees as he drove us down the pot-holed service road.

"Turned him into *what*?"

I shifted to look at Johnny, tearing my gaze away from the forest and the trees.

"A subject." *My queen.* "I think… I think I just made myself an alpha." I wanted to cry, to scream, but mostly I wanted to pound my chest and take ownership over what I'd done.

Johnny nodded like he already knew. He swallowed it whole, accepting that I'd claimed a pack as my own, then he grinned.

"I need to talk to Levi," I said, dread slipping into the awe.

* * * *

We were all in the library, Levi, Kane and Johnny watching me like hawks as I sorted through the parchments, moved the photos around, put them in order and saw them with new understanding. They told a different story than the one we'd assumed before.

"These wolves are her soldiers. We got that right." I pointed to the battle. I noted the streaks on their flesh, markings that spread from throats across chests, like the threads were reaching for the beast's hearts.

Levi shifted closer, inspecting the prints. "She marks them."

"The mark of the beast." Just like what I gave Gareth went unsaid. The heaviness of the room told me that everyone was thinking the same thing. I'd made him my soldier by biting him while I'd been in my werebeast form.

I pulled the series of prints out that showcased the orgy. "These are her mates."

Levi froze.

Kane moved closer.

Johnny stayed where he was, idlily scoping out a parchment on the other side of the table, one eyebrow now cocked.

"*She* gives the mating bite?" Kane reached for the print in my hand. I let him take it. Study it. Try to deny what I was now seeing so clearly. "With every intention comes a mark. With every mark comes a bond. With every bond comes a commitment," he read. "What the fuck does that mean?"

"I think we figured out why I was so against taking your bites." My beast wanted to build an army and a harem. Her agitation was unfulfilled instinct to strengthen her standing and her power.

Levi looked up, meeting my eyes, awe clearly etched on his face. "It's you who has to do the bonding. You select *your* mates. *You* create the link."

"My mating bite, in theory, would create the starburst pattern." I pointed to the markings on the men closest to the werebeast in the print. "Different from the soldiers." The ones closest to the queen had two puncture dimples the width of a beast's fangs then what looked like lightening streaks of white scar tissue unfurling around them. It was beautiful—and also terrifying.

Kane didn't tear his eyes away, but his chest was moving like he was taking some deep controlling breaths.

This was the moment of moments. Not only would Kane have to hand over his leadership, but he'd have to give me power over the mating bond if he truly wanted me to be queen. I didn't know what that would mean to him, but I guessed it wasn't all sunshine and roses in his brain right now. I didn't know what it would do, either. Gareth and his former pack were in my head — quiet now, thanks to my new-found control — but there all the same. It was a presence that comforted my beast, one that I was slowly getting used to…kind of.

It was definitely an emasculating prospect, considering how it'd always been done…with the male in control and doing the biting and claiming.

"And would you?" Johnny moved in next to me, close enough that his body heat came in waves to envelop me. He leaned his lips to my hair, his breath moving the strands when he spoke. "Would you bite each of us?" His words were sultry and soft, caressing my jaw, my throat. I froze, but not because I didn't want what he was offering.

Kane snapped his eyes to Levi's, then to Johnny's, then to mine. His expression was barely contained panic.

The air was ripe, palpable, so many emotions swirling…uncertainty shone in Kane's eyes like a pulse. I sucked in a breath, wobbled a little, suddenly off balance. I couldn't look at him and see vulnerability. It was too raw.

"Would it be too much still?" Levi asked, his usual all business tone gone, replaced by hope, desire, need. It slipped its way into my heart and made my brain fuzzy. "Would you rather choose one of us to form that kind of connection with? Or would you want us all?"

If there were ever a time for bated breath, it was now. It seemed like all three men were hanging on to my next words.

I don't know. I ran my fingers through my hair and put some distance between me and Johnny, pacing a short circuit.

"This is a lot." I wanted to sit down. I wanted to run.

I actually wanted to scream and cry and whine about how unfair this all was, but my beast roared within, a snap of her fangs on my conscious mind telling me to smarten up.

This is the way forward. A deeply instinctual calm fell over me. This was the way it would be done.

I straightened my spine and set my shoulders. Nothing had changed and yet everything had changed. My beast wanted this. *I* wanted this. I craved stability, and biting my uncle, taking his pack, had given me peace with her.

I jutted my chin then looked each of the men in the eye, one at a time.

"I won't pit you against one another." I kept my voice steady somehow. "I won't even consider doing this unless you're all on board with each other's decision. The question is, can you handle it?"

We all turned to face Kane.

He shifted his focus away, choosing to stare at the print instead, like he could make sense of this backward concept by glaring at the ancient picture. He ran his hand along the back of his neck then cleared his throat.

"Alpha Kane." Vic's voice cut through the tension.

Kane jerked his head toward the door.

"There's a call from Toronto. Came on the secure line." Vic scanned the room, frowned, obviously picked up on the tension in the room. He took a step back the way he came. "But I can get the details and pass a message along."

"No," Kane barked. He paused, collected himself with a slight shake of his shoulders, then put the print down gently. "No, I'm coming."

He left, and my questions hung like a noose.

Chapter Fifteen

Charlie

Kane was flustered, raking his fingers roughly through his hair and pacing in his den. I followed Johnny into Kane's sanctuary, knowing that the dynamic had altered between us. Suddenly, I was on equal footing, alpha to alpha, but the question still remained, would Kane accept my bite? Did I even want to give him one? For that matter, was I ready to bond with Johnny and Levi in such a permanent way?

Even though this was a complete and total mind-fuck of a twist, it also didn't feel wrong to me. Maybe Levi had been right all along, and females had been the ones with all the power, once upon a time.

My father always said there would be one queen to unite them all.

A fizz tingled down my spine then raced back up. *Maybe…maybe that really is supposed to be me.*

"We lost our lead on Andrew," Kane blurted, his eyes wild.

"What do you mean? I thought you said the men you had on it would get it done." I bit my tongue after those words slipped out.

Gareth provided us with coordinates and plans. His last contact with Andrew was the day of the attack on me. After that, Andrew went silent—presumably because he failed his mission and knew his life is in danger. Gareth sent some wolves to Toronto to hunt him. They were working for me now, taking my orders. Even still, Kane already had wolves on the ground in Toronto, and he had assured me that Andrew would be found.

Kane didn't give me one of his hard stares for the question, which was almost worse. To me that meant he knew he fucked up.

"They just called. Andrew vanished." Kane shook his head. "They were set to apprehend him, closed in on the alley he's been skulking for nights now. It should have been a done deal."

"Someone took him out?" Johnny offered, even though he didn't sound confident.

"His trail was cold. Dead cold." Kane sighed. "His scent was faint, like he hadn't been there at all."

"So, your guys lost him." I was frustrated. I wanted to do something about Andy myself. I knew Kane wouldn't approve—and that bothered me, not because I wouldn't go ahead and do it anyway, but because I wanted his approval. "Where did they track him? What alley was he haunting?" Maybe I could help position him. If he was near one of the few forest spaces in Toronto, I could give them an idea of prime hunkering locations.

"Close to your place. There was a large area of scent trail, but my guys were closing in." He lifted a shoulder. "West of your apartment, maybe four blocks?"

Fuuuuuck.

"I need to call Ruby." My heart was in my throat. "Make sure she's okay."

"Who the fuck is Ruby?" Kane asked.

Johnny shot him a what-the-fuck look before I could. "How do you not know who Ruby is?" He raised his hands when Kane glared. "What? Was I the only one keeping tabs on Charlie?"

I clocked that information. I'd take it up with Johnny later, *the spying bastard*, then hit Ruby's number on my phone. My stomach clenched, unease like poison.

"Hey, girl, what's up?" Ruby's voice was a balm to my nerves, and my anxiety deflated immediately. She sounded upbeat, healthy…happy, even.

"Nothing, just checking in." I couldn't help an edge of relief from whooshing out. "Still in Vancouver but missing you something fierce."

I really could use some girl time. Being surrounded by pulsating testosterone twenty-four seven was exhausting, and I needed guy advice from a girlfriend. Even if I couldn't tell her specifically what was going on, I would love to vent to her about the pressures of three men vying for my attention—or maybe not all three anymore. Doubt pummeled me now that the expectations had changed.

"Awww, I miss you, too." She clattered around the kitchen, knocking a few pots together before turning on the faucet. "Wish you were here."

The men were bickering about unauthorized surveillance and permission and spying. Kane may have been set on giving the first soul stripping to Johnny, but I planned on delivering the last.

I stepped into the hallway so I could chat in peace.

"Everything okay there?" It was a normal question, maybe a bit paranoid, but all the same, my stomach did a flip when she didn't answer right away.

"Well, define okay?" She laughed and I heard the muffled sound of her switching ears. "Nothing major. Kicked Jared out, finally. The kids are with his sister. She won custody, and he lost it."

I couldn't help the sigh that slipped out. I was worried she'd say she met Andy. I wouldn't put it past him to infiltrate my life in that way — use Ruby as a bargaining chip, seduce her or something. Werewolf males could be quite enticing.

Jared used his kids to hook Ruby when they first started dating. She was a total sucker for the single-dad love story, and he nailed her at Christmas. *Insert eye roll here.* He ticked all the boxes — gainfully employed, doting father, sweet and slightly damaged kids needing a mom. He swept her off her feet with grand gestures and made her fall for what could be — a readymade family.

It was definitely a case of too good to be true. Over the two years of them being together, he became more and more a loafer, lost his job, stopped doing his share of chores and childcare and turned into a burden and a drain on Ruby until he was no better than another child for her to care for. And she definitely hadn't signed up for that.

But she also had a big heart, and the kids didn't have anyone else to take care of them except for Jared's sister, who'd been fighting in court to take over custody and move them out east.

"How do you feel about that?" I knew it was complicated. As much as I wanted Ruby to be happy —

and being free of Jared was a clear, to me, path to happiness—I knew it meant Ruby was on her own again and lonely. She *did* love those kids, too, so it wasn't just the loss of a loafer boyfriend. I knew that a piece of her heart had gone when those kids left.

She shut off the water. "A bit sad. A bit relieved." Her voice caught. "The kids are where they belong. They'll have good lives with Jared's sister, surrounded by family. My place feels so empty and it's too quiet, but it's also nice." She forced a laugh. "I think I earned a girl's night out—or five."

It was a knife in the gut. Ruby, my first and only real friend, needed me, and I wasn't there for her. "I'm so sorry, Rubes. I should be there."

"Not trying to make you feel guilty for being away. I know you're dealing with family." She lightened her tone. "Once you get back, you've got a date with me."

"Deal!" Maybe I could bring her out here and set her up in a fancy hotel. Spend time with her in between Kane's torture sessions, Levi's research marathons and Johnny's whatevers. Then I remembered that I was alpha to a pack now, and my idea disintegrated.

Right. My life wasn't built for friendships outside of the pack, especially now.

A few moments of clattering pots and gushing water brought up an awkward pause. I knew Ruby was doing chores to keep busy. I didn't like that the tension over the phone was rising.

"Anything else going on?" My gut was all over the place.

She sighed. "It's just, things are weird right now." Another clang. "I'm worried I'll take Jared back because of the weirdness."

"Weird like *what*?"

I sensed Johnny stepping out from the den, checking in or spying? I shot him a dirty look. He winked but slipped back into the room. *Definitely checking in.*

I headed farther down the hall, bypassing the library, continuing to the bank of windows that overlooked the forest.

"Well, for one, I was being stalked by a coyote."

The blood froze in my body. My mouth went dry. My heart stopped. "What?"

"Yeah, like, this big brown coyote kept showing up in the alley next to the house. He'd be there when I put the garbage out. He'd be there when I walked anywhere. It was freaky."

"Ruby," I cut her off, "did he bite you?" *It's Andy.* He was stalking her. My heart sped up, racing like the finish line was seconds away.

She sputtered on a laugh. "No! Fuck no. I didn't get that close."

The spike of fear staking me slid out slowly. My heart eased its heavy thundering. "Thank fuck."

"He bit Jared." She laughed again. "But he deserved it, the ass."

My world tilted, knees wobbled, hands slicked with sweat immediately. Just as suddenly, my werebeast senses kicked into play, firming up my weakness so quickly that my rising panic flashed out and alpha mode took over.

"Tell me what happened," I ordered, my tone too rough, but Ruby didn't seem to notice.

"Jared was over picking up some of his stuff. The coyote was outside as usual. Jared tried to be all big tough guy, which we both know he isn't." She snorted. "The coyote dove for him. I screamed. Jared couldn't run fast enough back to the apartment. The coyote got him in the butt." She was laughing for real now, like this was some great comedy show. I knew she was expecting me to laugh with her, to take joy in Jared's mistake. In all other circumstances, the man would deserve a bite in the ass, but not this time.

"Where is he now?" My voice shook but I passed it off as a stunted laugh.

"Jared, oh he's —"

"The coyote. Where's the animal?" Ruby was in danger. I headed toward Kane's den.

I'd be flying back to Toronto immediately.

"Taken care of." She pulled the plug on the sink, and I heard water rushing down the pipes. "I called a wildlife officer. Coyote has been tranquilized, trapped and taken in for testing or something."

Oh fuck. Andrew was in human custody

"And Jared?" If he'd been bitten by a werewolf, his change would start immediately. He'd have until the full moon to adjust to the transformation before it completely took over, and given that it was only three days away, that meant that his shift was coming quickly — so quickly that it would most likely make him insane before it killed him.

Ruby started to answer when her doorbell rang. "Oh hey, speak of the devil."

It was late, close to midnight Toronto time.

My heart dropped to my toes.

"Ruby, don't answer the door."

But she wasn't listening.

"Charlie, hang on a sec." Her door squeaked open. "If you think a little ass injury is going to make me forgive you —"

Ruby screamed, and it was cut off in a gurgled way that made me nauseated.

"Ruby! Hang on. I'm coming."

I heard her phone hit the ground then the line went dead.

Chapter Sixteen

Kane

"I know where Andrew is," Charlie blurted, her face pale, eyes wide. "I have to get to Toronto."

She was talking so fast it was almost hard to follow her. "Toronto isn't safe, not with Andrew unaccounted for. You're an alpha now. You don't run into the danger."

"Don't even go there." She bypassed me on the way to the front door. "Ruby's in trouble."

I grabbed her arm, and she spun around, her teeth bared, werebeast right there, ready to rip my throat out. Somehow Charlie kept herself in check, and it was amazing to see...finally.

"Slow down. My men are there. I'll send them to Ruby. Just tell me what's going on."

She sucked in a deep breath, her eyes wild. "Her ex was bitten by Andy."

Three days until the full moon. He'd already be feeling the change like fire in his blood.

"He's at her apartment now. She screamed—" Charlie choked on a furious sounding sob.

"Give me an address." I'd already pulled my phone out.

Lex answered immediately, and I relayed the information Charlie gave me. It took less than ten seconds, but I knew Lex, Ari and Rue were on it. "They'll take care of it."

"Take care of it?" Like she was suspecting the men would hurt her friend, which, I would admit was protocol for some packs. If a human was accidentally bitten, chances were that human would disappear under mysterious circumstances, never to be seen again.

"They'll handle the ex and make sure your friend is okay." The ache in my chest was sudden and unnerving. It bothered me that she didn't trust me or even know me well enough to understand intuitively that I'd never do anything to hurt her—and, by extension, her friend.

But that kind of trust came from a bite, and my world had shifted where that was concerned.

"I'm going."

I knew there was no talking her out of it. "I'm coming with you." She might not be the alpha of the Duke clan, but she was destined to be, and I wasn't letting her go without backup.

"You're an alpha," Charlie said, her tone mocking as she repeated my words from earlier. "You don't run into the danger."

"If you're going, I'm going," I countered. Levi opened his mouth to argue but I cut him off. "You and

Johnny will stay here, monitor the situation and keep me posted."

"Fuck that, I'm coming," Johnny said, his expression one I knew well. If I didn't let him come with us, he'd show up on his own anyway. *Headstrong fool.*

Charlie moved to Johnny, her expression softening as she closed the distance between them. It made my heart spike like jealousy was a drug flooding my system. She put her hands on his cheeks, leaned up then kissed him tenderly, lingering long enough for the tension in the den to peak, and my desire to storm out of the room and punch some walls became unbearable. I looked at Levi, but he only had eyes for Charlie.

How could he watch this and not realize she was making a choice?

As she pulled away, she tilted her head so their foreheads touched, then she whispered, "I need you here with my uncle's—" She gulped. "*My* pack. Make sure they know what's happening. I've cut off their voices and their connection for my own sanity. Way too much noise. Make sure they're okay. Tell them to sit tight."

Johnny swallowed, his Adam's apple bobbing. I could tell that he wanted to argue but instead pulled back enough to nod. She'd made him her ambassador. She'd gotten him to listen, something I'd never been able to do with him.

"On one condition." He lifted his hands to cup her face. "Let's make this official before you go."

I couldn't believe those words, heavy with consequences, just came out of his mouth. Panic washed over me. I looked to Levi again, but he was nodding like this was all part of the plan. I whipped my gaze back to Charlie to see determination spread across her face.

"You're sure?"

Johnny nodded once, his eyes never leaving Charlie's

My world turned inside out. My chest constricted. *What is happening here?*

She wrapped her arms around his waist, hoisting herself up his body on tiptoes. He guided her face toward his throat as her fangs grew past her plump lips.

I opened my mouth to stop it—to tell them to take some time, think about it. We didn't even know what it would do to us. What if it made us mindless proles like Gareth?

Then I backpedaled on my own thoughts. Why would it? A mating bond was nothing like a pack bite. She wasn't creating werewolves in biting us. She was bonding with our entities. And yet...and yet...my gut wasn't right on this. It was beyond taboo. It broke all conventions.

I couldn't. I just couldn't. It should have been me marking *her*.

As her fangs sank into Johnny's neck, he sighed, and his eyelids fluttered closed. She moaned and right there in front of my eyes, a starburst formed, spreading across Johnny's skin. Dark, solid lines stretched from where her lips met his neck, up to his jaw and down below the collar of his shirt. Just like in the print. It was a moment from history come to life.

My mouth dropped open. My lungs froze. My heart pounded against my ribcage.

Johnny looked like a man in heaven. His eyes were hooded, his lips parted slightly and his body languid.

Charlie stepped back, leaving him to sway like he was in a trance.

This was all wrong. It was too fast. Too public. *No. No. No.*

She turned to Levi, stepping toward him and he to her. She kissed him passionately, lovingly. She didn't have to give him direction. He already knew his place.

This can't be happening.

"As much as I'd love to get in on the action, someone has to stay here to hold the fort." Levi sounded love lost, and he hadn't even taken her bite. "There's a car waiting, and the jet is on standby."

She nodded, reached up, caressed his jaw, tilted his head, her fangs glistening white. She licked their lengths, one then the other, mesmerizing in her sensuality. Then she nuzzled her lips into Levi's throat. As she sank her fangs into his skin, the knocking in my chest burned.

I blinked hard when the second starburst appeared.

It seemed too easy, but the marks were laden with consequences. I knew it, even if my brothers, even if Charlie, didn't.

She turned to me and every muscle in my body tensed. I took a step back, lifted my hands, shook my head. I couldn't. I *wouldn't* do this. It was all wrong…too rash. Not the way it was supposed to go.

I looked at Levi, then at Johnny, saw the satisfaction on their faces, and I felt isolated, alone. For the first time in our lives, my brothers had done something without me. Something huge. They'd taken a mating bond with no ceremony, like it was a common thing.

I bared my teeth, cringing at the idea of taking a bite so casually.

Angela Addams

When I looked at Charlie, I saw her hesitation. Hurt flashed over her face, there and gone in a second. Then her eyes held wisdom, understanding, acceptance. She knew. She'd always known.

"Let's go," she said to me, dismissing my rejection in a heartbeat—cold and decisive, just as an alpha should be.

She turned to the door and left me standing there with my heart in my throat and regret hanging in the air.

I looked at my brothers, who were both rubbing the new marks on their necks. They shared a grin and acted like this was a point of pride.

"Don't let it go to your heads," I barked. "You don't even know what it will do to you."

I frowned, shook my head, then I followed Charlie out of the door and barely stopped myself from punching a hole through the wall as I went.

Chapter Seventeen

Charlie

The silence was thick, and *fuck* and I'd love to be able to be anywhere else but with Kane on this tin-can plane. Okay, not exactly a tin can with the butter-soft leather seats, full food and beverage service and lavender-scented air that made me want to curl up and take a nap. There was probably even a bed in the back all ready for me to sleep my troubled thoughts away, though I hadn't explored.

The bite I gave to Levi and Johnny might have produced an instantaneous fizzy stomach, all-the-feels kind of connection and tattoo-like mark, but it was only now that the true implications of what I'd done were hitting home. It was impulsive of me to mark them so suddenly, acting on the desperate desire to stay connected to them while I was back in Toronto and the insistence of my beastly instincts. I'd never felt that kind of separation anxiety before, but when the barriers were removed and the path to Toronto open for me, I just didn't want to go without leaving a part of myself behind with my men.

My beastly instincts screamed to lay claim, and I hadn't seen any reason not to.

Now, the hooks of my decision had latched in, and I felt every pulse, every worry, every ounce of emotion from those two. I wanted to get off the flight and go back to the mansion. I wanted to be with them now, glued to their sides, never to be parted again.

I fought the urge to text or call, just to hear their voices, because I knew how crazy that would seem, and I never did crazy. At least now that my werebeast and I seemed to be one, I felt like crazy might push me over the edge to obsession territory.

The bombardment of emotions was overwhelming me to the point of panic. Levi and Johnny genuinely gave a shit about me, and while I'd kind of understood that in theory, now I had proof. I was connected on a soul level with both of them.

And yet, as much as it was threatening to drown me, I wouldn't even try to clamp down on the flood of emotions. It was the first time, since my father had died, that I felt loved, cherished, valued. I'd had no idea how much of a hole his passing had left in my heart.

So, I was marinating in Levi and Johnny's worry, knowing that it was amplifying my own trepidation about what I'd find in Toronto.

Two hours into the four-hour flight, I was dying for a distraction. I couldn't stop tapping my foot on the carpeted floor, my hand on my knee as I jittered like I'd had way too much caffeine.

And Kane...? He was just sitting there, directly across from me, staring at his hands like there was some kind of hidden message there for him to see.

His rejection stung. It more than stung. It was a blade to the heart, and I was trying to reconcile why. My sudden change of mind, accepting the reality that there was something inside me that knew I had a destiny with these men, giving the bite, making it official in so much as blood was spilled, it was spur of the moment. When Johnny asked, I'd felt compelled to do it. I knew Kane would have some reservations but to reject me outright? Even with the evidence right in front of him. Those starbursts...

"You know, you're clinging to the patriarchy like it's a life raft," I blurted, stunned by my own words. I clamped my mouth shut, glaring out of the window like it would save me from myself, silently cursing the word vomit that I spewed.

I could practically feel Kane's hard gaze on me. I expected a blast of his temper, a lashing with his wicked tongue. What I got instead cooled my inner rage instantly.

"It's too sudden. I'm not ready." He sounded reasonable, calm, so I dared a peek at him and found his eyes like lava, burning with intensity. He was as conflicted as I was. It was right there in his furrowed brow and tense jaw.

"You said I was destined to be alpha with you as my second, by my side." I was riled all over again by his composure. How dare he be so calm! "Now I'm agreeing to bonding, and you're backing away."

"This isn't how I envisioned it," he said simply, with a shrug to punctuate, as if that was all it'd take to satisfy me.

"Right — the way *you* envisioned it. You marking me. Me subservient to you." I crossed my arms, ready to glare out of the window all over again.

"Is that really how you think the mating bond works?" He pushed himself to the edge of his recliner then leaned forward, forcing me to focus on him and only him. "Is that really how you think *I* work?"

My mouth gaped, my thoughts instantly shifted to my dreams and the span of his fingers across my ass. My cheeks heated. "Um…that's exactly what you're — "

He gripped the back of my head and pulled me close. His eyes swallowed me. His scent tickled the back of my throat and made my mouth water. His heat blasted the cold in my heart, blowing my anger away in an instant. "In the bedroom, yes, I will always dominate." He nipped my bottom lip, and I melted, oozing desire out of every pore. "On the training field, yes, I will push you, demand more." He kissed along my jaw, and I shivered, jolts zinging along my nerve endings. "But not as my mate."

My brain was on fire. My body ready to blaze. I leaned closer, wanting so badly to climb into the seat with him. "Then it shouldn't matter how it happens," I whispered, my voice rough.

He pulled back with a sigh, breaking the spell between us so suddenly that I almost tumbled forward. "You don't understand."

He looked out of the window, and I quickly righted myself, embarrassed all over again for almost face planting in his lap.

"When we were pups, our mother would tell us about these fantastical creatures, female warriors who led fiercely and commanded loyalty." I'd heard this story already, but there was something in his tone that kept me quiet. "She told us that there was a prophecy about the rise of a female champion, one who was whispered about among the other females. She was coming. Actually, my mother believed she was already born and destined to change our world for the better — a savior for every female who had been neglected, abused, murdered." He ran his fingers through his hair, still staring out of the window. I knew this was easier for him, but I wanted him to look at me while he was telling me about my destiny. "She told me that it could be my destiny to bond with this warrior. That if I devoted myself to building my strength and my power, I would be the one to bolster her, protect her flank, stand at her side."

Look at me!

This was important. It was meaningful to him. He was staring at the clouds when he should have been staring at me. I was supposedly his queen and yet...the sinking sensation in my gut told me that I'd blown it. I'd changed the story. My bite wasn't part of his plan. It wasn't what he'd built his life toward. In one spontaneous moment, I'd shattered his dreams.

And there was more...

"When I told her that wasn't the way things were done, that it was the other way around, the female would support the male, she'd looked at me sternly and said that my bite would ignite an unstoppable change, that it was vital for the other males to see my mark on the warrior queen's skin so that they would know that *my* claim, while absolute, would be all the more meaningful when I stepped out of the way of her, my warrior queen, and supported her rule."

Fuuuck. His words sank like a boulder in my gut.

"So, you see, if you mark me, you'll gain control over the pack, yes…" He finally turned his head so that our eyes met. His weren't on fire anymore. They were subdued…withdrawn. "But I fear that you'll set the Duke clan up in the eyes of the other packs as weak."

"So, they'll underestimate us then we'll show them we're *not* weak!" I tried for cheerleader and sounded about as pathetic as I felt.

I'd fucked this up for Kane. I'd destroyed his dream, and I was asking him to rewrite his destiny. No matter what, I still couldn't agree to his bite. I couldn't. It was against everything I'd ever believed. So fitting that I found a man who shared the same dogmatic beliefs about the way of our worlds but he was on the opposite side of the spectrum.

"Charlie, we live in a world dominated by powerful men. All I'm saying is that it might make sense to meet them in their world first, then yank them into a new one — not for the sake of the alphas who you can clobber and bite into submission, but for the pack you adopt who you won't bite, who come to you by proxy. We're talking thousands of wolves potentially. You can't mark them all."

I wanted to argue, but I knew he was right. He'd been thinking strategy, and I'd been working on emotion.

"I'm not trying to perpetuate the male dominance narrative, but my bite carries weight. I've made sure of that, and it's meant — has always been meant — to bolster you. I can't turn my back on that concept, not even in the face of ancient evidence that suggests the mark needs to be reversed. I just…don't feel like we have the full story." He turned back to the window, shutting me out again. "So, I say again, I'm not ready. It's too much for me to accept right now."

The silence hung once more. The pit in my stomach grew. I'd marked Levi and Johnny. Had I made them vulnerable by ignoring the legacy of power that the patriarchy held? Had I ignored the natural laws of our kind, somehow?

No. My gut said no. Just because it wasn't how Kane pictured didn't make it wrong. And yet, his words rang true. There was something to be said for playing the game as it was meant to be played then hitting them when they least expected it.

I leaned my head against my hand and turned my gaze back out of the window. Heavy thoughts circled my brain, threatening to pull me under.

My gut said he wasn't wrong—but he wasn't right, either.

Chapter Eighteen

Charlie

We landed in Toronto and got to Ruby's house as quickly as possible, which was pretty fast, given that Levi had arranged everything once we landed. There was no scrambling to find a car or dealing with traffic, because the driver of our SUV knew all the ways to bypass congestion and got us to Ruby's place in record time.

Kane was updated repeatedly on the flight about the situation on the ground. Jared had been dealt with. I wasn't asking how, but I had a feeling he wouldn't be showing up on Toronto streets ever again. It was brutal, but whatever they did to him would have been far more humane than what he was heading toward as the full moon grew closer.

Ruby, thank fuck, was secured. So, when I barged into her small apartment, I was amped up, yes, but not in a scared-for-my-friend's-life kind of way. It was more like a fuck, how am I going to explain this sort of thing.

Ruby was in the kitchen, cooking up a storm when I burst into the compact room. She had a spatula in her hand, bacon frying on the stove, pancakes on a countertop griddle and three huge men hunkered down at the crammed table, shoveling food into their mouths like they'd never seen it before.

"Charlie!" Ruby cheered. Her long hair was in a topknot, her bangs parted in a haphazard kind of way. She had a sheen of sweat on her forehead, and her cheeks glowed pink. The kitchen was warm and oozing with smells that made my mouth water. "These friends of yours are bottomless pits! I've made a million pancakes already."

"This is the best food I've had in decades," Lex said with his mouth full of everything. "Seriously, woman, you're a master chef."

She was grinning so hard her face looked like it was about to split, and her eyes sparkled like I hadn't seen in a long time. I squeezed into her space and gave her a big hug, soaking in her cinnamon scent and familiar embrace. There was nothing like having a friend like Ruby—no obligations, no wolfie protocols or expectations, just love and acceptance.

"You're okay? Jared didn't hurt you?" I gulped around the lump in my throat, still unsure how I was going to break it to Ruby that Jared wouldn't be coming back *ever*. He might have been her ex, but I knew Ruby well enough to suspect she'd be looking out for him once she got past their breakup. She cared, maybe too much, about everyone in her life, past and present.

Ruby laughed. "Hell no. I kneed him in the nuts and ripped out a chunk of his hair right as these guys showed up, saying they were friends of yours." She leaned closer then whispered, "Where were you hiding these hunks, Charlie? Seriously, they're gorgeous."

I heard a chuckle and knew that the gorgeous hunks had heard Ruby, despite her attempt to keep it quiet. I pulled back and gave her a once-over, making double sure she was unhurt before I turned to the three at the table. "Thanks for getting here so quickly."

Lex nodded, his mouth still full.

"We were in the neighborhood," Ari said with a nod at Kane as he eased himself through the kitchen door.

I felt Ruby stiffen for a second before she turned on her usual hospitality. "Wow, another giant." She laughed. "What do they feed you guys in Vancouver?"

"Ruby, this is Kane Duke." I stepped back to give Ruby some space. "He's a...friend of mine from back home."

Kane offered his hand. Ruby studied me for half a second, one eyebrow cocked, before turning to Kane with another huge grin. "Sit down. There's room." She waved his hand away and patted him on the arm instead. "I bet you're hungry, too, right?"

Much to my surprise, Kane did what Ruby said and settled himself in the last seat at the table. He and his men exchanged some meaningful looks, but otherwise the focus was on the food that Ruby doled out, keeping plates full for the guys. She had no idea what kind of damage a single werewolf could do to her pantry, but she seemed to be completely in love with the idea of filling these guys up.

"Can you pour me a coffee?" Ruby nodded toward the coffee maker. "I just brewed a fresh pot."

I noted the nervous tic of her cheek and realized that as much as she was thriving in culinary bliss, she had questions, and we needed some time alone. I owed her explanations, and I knew she expected the truth. My stomach was in knots, because I was unsure what to safely tell her.

I did as she'd asked, pouring both of us a cup, then fixing hers the way she liked it. With two coffees in hand, I nodded to the table of men. "Hey, guys, I'm going to steal your chef for a few. How about one of you take over cooking duties for now?"

Ruby didn't argue. She laid the spatula down. "The bacon is almost ready, and the pancakes just need a flip in a minute."

Leaving the warmth and intensely delicious smells of the kitchen was heartbreaking. I'd much rather sit down and feast like the rest of the pack, but Ruby deserved some truths, even if I couldn't tell her all of them.

"You didn't have to drop everything and run to my rescue." Ruby slipped her arm into the crook of mine and nudged me with her shoulder once we were through the tight hall and into her cozy living room. "I had things under control." Her voice wavered. "Mostly…I mean. It was a little crazy the way Jared was acting."

I set the cups down on the coffee table then pulled Ruby into another hug. "I'm so sorry I wasn't here for you."

The tension left her body in an instant, and she wrapped me up in her arms too.

"Don't be silly. You had things going on."

I pulled back to look at her face. Her eyes were swimming a little, and I knew she was fighting a torrent. "I'm sorry this happened to you."

It's my fault.

I clamped down on my guilt. There was no point blurting things I couldn't explain to her. I didn't want to put her life in danger with any information that wasn't absolutely necessary. A human knowing about the existence of werewolves came with a price I wasn't willing to make Ruby pay.

"Nothing for you to be sorry about." Ruby patted her cheeks, wiped her fingers under her eyes to catch some tears then put on her megawatt smile. "I'm just glad you're here."

She steered me toward my usual spot on the couch then slid herself into her place, legs up, our toes touching, just as things used to be — with the exception, of course, that four werewolves were sitting in the other room, likely listening to everything we said.

"So, you going to tell me who the hunks really are or what?" Ruby blew on her coffee, even though I'd put enough cream in it to drown out any heat, then took a sip. "I know you have no friends except yours truly, so..."

I jabbed her butt with my foot and laughed along with her, my own coffee cup in hand, the smell of Ruby's favorite hazelnut blend making me feel right at home.

Fuck, I missed this.

"I've known Kane for a long time." I stuck as close to the truth as possible. "Friend of the family. Just hadn't seen him for a while." I shrugged. "We reconnected back home."

"Reconnected?" Ruby gave me an exaggerated wink. "I'd love to hear the dirty details of that."

My cheeks heated instantly, and Ruby giggled. "That good, huh?"

"No, no...nothing like that." Okay, exactly like that, but not the way she thought, obviously.

"Sure, sure. He's capital H hot, Chuck. Seriously!" She fanned herself. "Those guys in there are built like my wildest fantasy men combined. I nearly choked on all the testosterone. And when they came barreling into my place like superheroes? Damn, I thought I was hallucinating."

There was an undercurrent to her words that made my smile falter. She was riding an edge right now, going along with things to keep her sanity. Underneath it all, she was crumbling. My world and what it came with could drown even the strongest human.

"I freaked out when you screamed," I said as I sipped my coffee. "Kane knew they were in the area, so he made a call. No big deal. I'm just glad you're okay."

Ruby set her cup down then rubbed her arms. "Yeah, it's just weird, you know? For Jared to act that way. He was always a lazy ass, but he was never violent. I probably should call the cops or something, but Lex told me they'd make sure Jared understood not to come back." She shivered, all trace of humor gone from her face. "They said they wouldn't hurt him."

They lied.

"You didn't fly here just for me, though, did you?" She screwed her face up. "I didn't pull you away from your family business, did I?"

I started to shake my head then realized Ruby would see through my bullshit in a heartbeat. "I was freaked out, Rubes. I heard you scream. I wasn't here for you." I put my cup down. "But yes, I have things to settle here, too."

"To settle, as in you're staying in Vancouver, aren't you?"

I didn't come here with the intention of shutting down my life in Toronto, but now that I was here, I knew my presence would only put Ruby in danger again and again. I nodded, fighting the urge to blurt the truth and beg Ruby to come with me.

She rubbed her thumb, circling her cuticle over and over, her eyes downcast. "Fuck, that really sucks."

"Why don't you come back with us?" Even as I said it, I knew she couldn't. "You can stay for a while. Take a vacation."

"What? And leave my dream job?" Ruby smiled sadly. "I don't exactly get vacation time."

"Yeah." If I was truly alpha of the Duke clan, the only pack I'd feel confident wouldn't totally mess Ruby up, I could set her up in a place, pay her bills and find a safe job for her to do for the pack. She'd see right through it. Which meant, she'd have to pledge allegiance and that would come with all kinds of truths that I couldn't and wouldn't force on her. It would change her in many ways, harden the parts of her that I loved.

"I guess you have to take those three guys back with you, right?" She cracked a smile. "It wouldn't be my luck that they'd live here." She rubbed her thumb again, frowning a little as she did. "I can handle three guys, don't you think?"

"Three at once?" I laughed. "Hell yeah." I frowned as she continued to rub her thumb. "What's up with your hand? You burn yourself or something?"

Ruby looked down at her thumb, then back up at me. "Nah, just a scratch."

I moved closer, shifting my legs to the floor then inspected her thumb. There was a red streak and a divot that extended from her cuticle to her first knuckle. "How'd you do that? Looks sore."

"It's nothing." She waved my concern away then picked up her cup again. "Like I said, things with Jared went crazy, fast."

I froze, my own cup midway to my mouth.

"He actually tried to bite me. Got my hand in his mouth." She laughed. "Imagine if I got rabies or something from my ex."

My world stopped. My breath came out so hard that my coffee sprayed.

"He broke skin? With his teeth?" I dropped my cup back to the table then snatched her hand again. "Fuck."

"Not a big deal. Seriously." Ruby tried to laugh it off. "It's just itchy as hell."

"What's wrong?" Kane said, filling the door with his huge body, his tone all business.

I locked eyes with him. "Ruby's been bitten."

Chapter Nineteen

Johnny

Like hell I was staying home while Kane and Charlie flew off to Toronto. Levi had things under control – he always did – and I was going to make sure the Andrew situation was dealt with properly. Charlie wanted him badly. I felt her desire to tear a strip into him, both figuratively and literally. It was my duty to satiate her needs, and I planned to do that in every way.

Her bite was no joke. I couldn't stop tracing the lines of the starburst on my throat. It pulsated like a drumbeat and radiated heat that was almost too much to endure. I'd been branded, and with every minute that passed, it felt like threads were weaving into my skin, connecting directly to Charlie's essence – to her thoughts, to her feelings, to her heart and soul.

I made a few calls to my boots on the ground in Toronto as I was heading to my chartered plane. I didn't have access to the Duke jet, obviously, since

Charlie and Kane were already boarded and taxing on the runway, but I had my own means of securing transportation.

"Hey, Johnny, how's it hanging?" Kent, a good friend and pilot always in need of extra cash, continued his pre-flight check.

"It's not hanging, bro. It's hard as a rock and ready for some fun."

Kent laughed and shook his head. "So, this is an emergency cock run?"

"I need to get to Toronto fast, and I know you can make that happen." I slapped him on the back. Kent was human, so I went easy. Didn't want to knock him to the ground out cold and mess up my chance to catch up with Charlie.

"You're damn right. I have a need for speed." He finished what he was doing then motioned to the stairs. "You got some new ink?"

I dropped my hand from my neck, realizing that I'd been stroking my link to Charlie the whole time. "Yeah, dude. Got it from my girl."

"I've heard ink like that is the kiss of death for relationships, man. Tread carefully." He closed the door behind us, and I couldn't help but feel his warning like an ominous prophecy.

I fought the urge to touch my neck again, even though the desperation to be close to Charlie flared, burning like her bite was alive. I wasn't being reckless, and I wasn't endangering my new bond. I was being proactive and getting the job done. No need to second guess myself at this stage.

I waved him off and took a seat, anxious to get into the air and on my way to my mate.

"Buckle up, buddy!" Kent disappeared into the cockpit, and I slid into my seat.

Just before takeoff, I got a string of texts from my guys in Toronto. Andrew was locked up in an enclosure at a wildlife center. The only reason he hadn't been euthanized was because the humans wanted to study him. They'd already figured out that he was different, and that was bad news for our kind. Andrew knew this, too, and he was going to be desperate to find a way out of lock up before mercenaries came to get him or the humans cut him open for a look-see. A desperate wolf was a very bad thing. It might make him so reckless that he went into werewolf mode to get free, and that, for sure, would attract way too much human attention, not to mention a bloody massacre.

My guys were working out a way to get to him first. *I want him alive*, I typed. *And talking*.

Because if there was one thing I knew for sure, Andrew was stalking Ruby for a reason, and that reason was, for sure, connected to Sal. My gut said that Charlie was in danger. I knew she could handle things herself, but I was her mate now and I had a duty to make sure her back was protected at all times. Kane might be with her, but he didn't take her mark, so he didn't know what the beat of her heart felt like etched into his skin. He didn't know what it meant to be one with Charlie.

* * * *

The wildlife center was located just east of the city, which took me farther away from Charlie than I wanted to be.

Couldn't be avoided, though.

Standard protocol for human captured werewolves was to terminate them. Sal would send his men to do that as soon as he found out Andrew had been caught. I needed to secure Andrew before he was killed, because Charlie wanted to grill him and so did I. The giant turd had information that we wanted, I was sure of it.

The sun was setting as my Uber reached the sanctuary, and the scent in the air reeked of werewolves.

My phone dinged. *Heads up, Johnny.*

My guys were waiting in a dark SUV on the edge of the parking lot. As they piled out to greet me and I waved away my Uber driver, I knew the wafting smell of monsters wasn't coming from them, so better for the human to get as far away as quickly as possible.

"We've got company." I embraced my guys, ferals turned by me over twenty years ago when I needed to make a mark in our world. It wasn't taboo or unheard of for lieutenants of a pack to create their own *small* team, but I'd kept these three a secret from everyone, even Kane and Levi. They were my henchmen, loyal to me and now, by proxy, to Charlie.

"Yeah, we clocked them already," Devon said with a nod toward the back of the building in front of us. "Don't think they know we're here, and if they do, they don't seem to care. Up until ten minutes ago, we were watching them work out a way to break your guy out of the sanctuary. Figured we'd let them do the hard work and swoop in to take their prize."

"They putting a plan into action now?" I took another sniff of the air, and something in my gut told me Devon was wrong.

"Yeah, they've killed the power to the fence and moved around back. My ears tell me they're cutting through the fence as we speak." Devon had an uncanny ability to pick up on the minutest of sounds. While I couldn't hear anything beyond the rustling of the forest, I trusted he was right, and they were minutes away from getting our prize.

My hackles were up, all the same. The forest didn't sound totally right either, though. There was something vibing our way that made my jaw tight. It wasn't the wolves breaking into the perimeter fence we needed to worry about. I scanned the darkened area of the trees. Nothing to see there.

"Any other security on site?" I pulled my stare away from the tree line to study the building.

"Already taken care of." Pete shrugged when I looked his way. "Whoever these guys are, they took out the night guard already. Not a death blow but the guy won't be getting up anytime soon."

Not a death blow? These were not Sal's guys for sure, then. I scanned the forest one more time... Out there was another story.

"We need to speed this up. Assume these guys are friendlies, likely sent by Kane or Gareth. Time to introduce ourselves and get Andrew out of there."

Sal's guys were here — watching, waiting, definitely stalking. They were staying back while all the work was done for them, just like my guys had been planning. I noted the expansive wide open parking lot. If we needed to battle, I didn't want it to happen in the open. I turned to the fence in the distance that encircled the sanctuary where our primal brethren — wolves, coyotes, foxes — were being cared for. If we had to battle, I wanted it to happen inside the fence.

I had an idea.

I motioned to Pete to take the flank and keep watch while Devon, Keith and I jogged around the back of the building toward the sound of metal crunching metal. Now that I was within range, the sound was unmistakable.

The others shifted to wolves, moving stealthily toward the racket, then fanned out to surround the werewolves who were attempting to cut through the wire.

I lifted my hands as I purposely stepped on a branch, alerting the other men of my presence.

"We come in peace." I flashed one of my more charming smiles, which did nothing to disarm the weres in front of me.

Two instantly dropped to all fours, shifting from men to beasts in a flash. The two others leveled guns that I could only assume were loaded with silver.

My guys were just behind, hunkering low and keeping their scents downwind.

"Kane send you?" I watched as their faces registered surprise, followed quickly by suspicion. "You all formerly with Gareth's pack?" *Now with Charlie* went without saying.

"Who's asking?" The bigger of the two barked with a nod to his gun.

"Johnny Duke. We're on the same side." I motioned over my shoulder. "As much as I'd love to get to know you all, Sal Larsen's mercs are closing in. We've got maybe two minutes to fetch our target before the bad guys try to put us all out of our miseries."

The two with the guns exchanged looks.

"Our alpha told us to bring Andrew to her and Kane. She didn't say anything about you being here." The guy talking lowered his gun slightly, as if not quite ready to believe me.

I brandished my throat, pointing to my tattoo. "She's my alpha, too, now…and my mate. Charlie wants Andrew alive for questioning, and I'm here to make sure it happens. Consider me backup." I waved my men forward.

They skulked out of the trees, muzzles to the ground, eyes alert.

"Now, like I said, Sal's thugs are here, and they want blood. I'd prefer it not be ours."

As if my words were enough to conjure them, a dozen beefed-up, armed-to-the-teeth henchmen came strolling out from the parking lot. "Well, well, I see we're just in time for a party. Johnny Duke, what the devil are you doing here?" Wade Johnson, one of Sal's better-known soldiers for hire turned Larsen lieutenant, was leading the pack. He was as badass as they came — shoot to kill then disembowel for good measure, all without breaking a sweat. "I know Sal doesn't have you on the payroll."

"Nope, not working for Sal. But how about we take care of this little problem for you. Save you the trouble of getting your muzzles all bloody." I knew negotiating with these guys was going to get me nowhere, but Devon and Pete had already slipped into the sanctuary along with two of Charlie's guys. I needed to buy them some time to find Andrew.

"You know that's not how this is going to go down, Johnny." He slid his gun into a holster on his chest. "But we don't need things to get nasty, either. How about you and your guys head back to your vehicle and leave the hard work for us. We'll show you the body as a courtesy. I know how Kane likes to maintain law and order, but the bounty is ours."

I frowned, realizing that Wade thought Kane was working as sheriff to our kind, a role he once did aspire to, way before he became the alpha he was today. What did that make me? His deputy? I stifled a snort. These guys had no idea how powerful Kane was, how much he'd amassed to date. Which meant that their boss, Sal Larsen, was also under the delusion that the Duke clan was scrambling to secure a place among the elite of our kind, not realizing, of course, that we were already there.

"Well, you know how Kane gets with the rules." I played it up, hardly able to contain my smirk. "I've got some questions for Andrew before you take him out."

Wade scratched his chin, frowned then shook his head. "Can't allow that, I'm afraid. Sal was very clear...no talking, just head detachment." He drew his gun again. "You understand, of course. Justice comes first when it's about exposure. We'd be willing to let you do the cleanup. Take care of the security guard and scrub the place for evidence. Sal will throw you some cash." He rested one hand on his second holster like this was a casual conversation. Trying to let me know he wasn't intimidated by me but really, his gesture meant he totally was. "But the target is a dead man."

"That's a generous offer, Wade." I sighed and rubbed my hand over the back of my neck. "But that's not going to work for me. I need the guy alive."

"I guess we have a problem after all, then, don't we?" He pulled his second gun then pointed it at my chest while he aimed the other in the general direction of my backup. "I don't want trouble, Johnny, but if you get between me and my bounty, I'll have to put you down, too. You know how the law goes."

Finders keepers.

"I'd like to see you try." A ripple of something unfamiliar coursed through me, vibrating my muscles like a spasm.

Charlie.

Fear spiked down my spine, painful and fast, ripping at my nerve endings. The threads binding me to my mate flared alive like they hadn't been before, setting my whole body on fire with adrenaline.

Charlie's fear ignited my instincts, and for the first time in my werewolf life, I knew that I was going to lose control over my wolf.

"Give me everything you've got," I roared.

Things were going to get bloody.

Chapter Twenty

Charlie

I managed to stay calm.

Calm enough to sweet talk Ruby to agree to an all-expenses trip with me to Vancouver. Calm while she called her boss and demanded the vacation time she was owed. Calm enough to help her pack and smile the whole time she gushed about hanging with my hunky friends. I was even calm as she harassed me over my ridiculous freak out because of her scratch.

"Jared's version of a parting gift," she'd laughed. *"It didn't even bleed…much,"* she'd teased.

I stayed calm right up until the fever kicked in and Ruby's eyes rolled to the back of her head. She almost hit the floor like a sack of potatoes.

Almost, but I caught her, saving her head from bashing into the corner of her dresser.

"Kane, I need you!" His thundering steps roared up the stairs, followed closely behind by Lex.

Both men looked as frantic as I felt. I laid Ruby down on her bed, helpless as her body started to shake. I'd hoped we'd get her to the plane at least, but the way werewolf bites worked was unpredictable...until they weren't. Now that the symptoms had started, we knew what lay ahead for Ruby — pain, suffering and death.

"Roll her on her side," Kane ordered, moving into the cramped space to help me get Ruby over.

Her body seized, arms and legs rigid. I climbed onto the bed with her, shifting in behind so I could brace her, cradling her body like I could stop the transformation. "She's burning up." Heat wafted off her like she was a furnace. Sweat already soaked her hair.

Her head lashed back, almost taking me out with the violence of it, then she was shaking again, every limb, every muscle, spasming like an earthquake. She cried out, keening like a wounded animal.

"I'm here, Ruby. It's going to be okay," I lied, desperate to reassure her. I held tight, trying not to smother her but needing Ruby to feel me there. "I'm going to get you help."

As if my words were enough to stop her seizure, the shaking tapered off and Ruby's body deflated into limp noodles. She moaned. Her eyes fluttered but her breathing grew steady.

"If we're going to move her, now is the time." Kane's voice was gruff. When I looked up at him sharply, he added, "We can't help her here. We need Levi. He'll know what to do."

Chapter Twenty-One

Johnny

I was rabid…furious. There was blood everywhere, and I couldn't tell if it was mine or theirs. I didn't care, either.

I was a beast, and I wanted blood.

I'd locked Charlie out. I didn't want her sensing the change in me. Everything was instinctive — the drive to kill, to complete my mission and achieve my alpha's goals. My mate didn't need the burden of the bloodbath or my fury.

I wasn't a wolf, not in this moment. I had arms and legs, and I was towering over the men surrounding me. I was a werebeast full of power.

Like Charlie, my mate.

Wade shot me twice. I felt the silver sear into my flesh, splitting open organs, wounds that should have killed me but didn't. I didn't know what Charlie's mark had done to me, but I was feral and, seemingly, invincible.

I ripped his arm from his body, taking the weapon with it, making it useless against me.

He wailed, screamed, clenched his gaping wound, his face full of terror. I didn't make him suffer. His head detached easily, and I used it as a weapon, aiming at his next in command, a wolf growling and nipping at my shins. *Just a nuisance.* I took him out with Wade's thick skull, hitting so hard that the wolf flew away, soaring into the trees until I couldn't see where he landed. By the sound of the crunch, I knew he wouldn't be coming back, though.

More shots were fired. More burning like beestings. I marveled at my new defenses…my new strength. I felt like nothing could stop me. Nothing would keep me from completing my mission.

The men surrounding me, werewolves who should have given me a fight, were nothing to me now.

I swiped my claws and gnarled into muscle, sinew and bone. I ripped out hearts and tore more limbs free. I disemboweled. I destroyed. I gutted and killed.

I was a monster.

"Johnny!" A familiar voice roared into my head, pulling me from the insane lust for blood. "They're dead."

The blood haze lifted. I was sucking in gore as I breathed through my mouth, spraying blood in a mist when I exhaled. There were dead bodies everywhere. Blood and body parts were strewn over the lot.

Our enemy was no longer a threat.

My men stood before me. Charlie's men did the same, with them Andrew, cowering like he should be.

They were all scared. I could smell their fear.

I want to tell them they were safe from my wrath, but I couldn't get my words to form. My throat was clogged. My head hurt with drilling pain that flashed down my spine and made me stumble.

"Whoa! Johnny, it's done. Easy, dude. You can calm down now." Devon approached with his hands out, moving slowly, caging a wild animal. "You with me, man?"

I hunched over and realized I was back in my human form, covered in blood, my clothing layered over top of the evidence of my massacre.

"What happened—?" Another lash of pain ripped down my body, and I crumpled to my knees.

"You freaked out, man," Keith said, with more than a little awe in his voice. "I've never seen anything like it. You were a beast…unstoppable."

No one came to my side. Everyone held back enough to let me know I'd obliterated their trust. I'd beasted out, just like Charlie. I'd lost control.

"I made a mess." I tried for a joke that fell flat as the pain gripped my gut and sent me keeling over. I hit the concrete, my head bouncing off the hard surface. Curled up in a ball, shaking with spasms, I couldn't control what happened next, but I knew where I needed to go. "Get me to Levi. There's something wrong with me. He'll know what to do."

I hope.

Chapter Twenty-Two

Charlie

My body, exhausted from everything that had happened, soaked into the cushions of the butter-soft leather lounge chair on the jet. My eyelids were weighted, impossible to keep open. Second-by-second, my muscles released enough to push me into darkness and relieve me from the immediate stress of getting Ruby to you.

The veils of shadows caressed my skin, soothing in a way I'd never appreciated until now.

This was a safe place for me to regroup, to unwind.

I didn't want to be alone.

It was my desire for your comfort, your strength and reassurance, that called you into my mind. My need for both you and Johnny, now my bonded mates, was palpable.

When you slid out of the shadows, you were a wolf with cunning, hungry eyes. Your fangs gleamed and your lips curled. I ran my fingers through your silky fur, trailing down your spine to your tail. Something primal zinged through my body, a knowing that you were mine, that I had claimed you.

You turned to rub along the backs of my legs before giving my wrist a long lick. I shivered as I laid my hand on your head and stared at your upturned face, wondering why you hadn't turned into your human form.

Shift for me.

I needed to talk.

I needed your guidance.

Johnny appeared behind you, his usual wry wolfie expression replaced by narrowed eyes and bared fangs. He growled a warning. That primal part of me, my beast side, came online, perking up at the sound. My gut instinct alerted to danger and goosebumps rose.

"What's wrong?" Spikes of anxiety jabbed me enough to dissolve the shadows around us. "Tell me."

My worry shifted from Ruby to you both, knowing that something was off. A ripple went over your body, muscles tensing, agony contorting your muzzle so you looked ferocious. Fear was a hot poker, jabbing me from all sides, not for my safety but for yours.

Johnny's body shook as he lifted himself onto hind legs, his torso shifting without completion, somewhere stuck between wolf and human. His skin rippled, waves tearing him apart. He clawed at his throat, leaving gouges that closed as fast as they opened. Silent screams stretched his jaw wide.

He teetered over to land hard on his back, rumbling the shadow ground, sending fog out like a tsunami. Horror gripped my heart.

"Levi." I sputtered over my next words, my voice an echo that got sucked away into the shadows. You were no longer at my side.

You stretched your body, front legs angled down, paws with fingers ending in claws. Your spine contorted, undulating in a great arch, then curving until your hind legs gave out. You were stuck, too. You dug your muzzle into your side, frantically biting at your flesh as if that would help ease your shift. You whimpered and growled, shredding my heart with each sound.

You were both struggling to transition but meeting resistance that I couldn't see. Flashes of human skin sprouted fur then rolled back to flesh, showing your tattoos had expanded, the starburst stretching well beyond my initial bite.

I zeroed in on the threads that bound us and tried to coax your shift forward, to give you peace and bolster your power, but my primal instincts told me something was missing, something obvious that I wasn't seeing. I coaxed my beast forward, wishing she would take over, help me figure this out, but we were melded now. We shared one mind, and something was blocking me from knowing what to do. My horror was her horror. She didn't have a suggestion or a path forward.

Johnny writhed on the ground, shadows teasing his flesh as he fought against whatever was working against him.

You turned your knowing eyes to me, blue clouded with storms, and it was obvious then that whatever was happening to you both was my fault.

Chapter Twenty-Three

Charlie

I woke on a gasp, my eyes wide, body full of terror. "Something is wrong with Levi and Johnny!"

Kane was frowning at his phone as he punched the screen with his thick fingers. "I know. He's cycling through transitions." He lifted his cell to his ear and speared me with a hard glare, letting me know that he was aware I was the cause of this problem. "Johnny's not answering."

"Isn't he with Levi?" But I knew even as I said it that he wasn't. *Shit. Shit. Shit!* He'd come after me. I should have known. I should have been paying attention to him, to Levi instead of being solely focused on Ruby. I was alpha now and a bonded mate, so I should have known what was happening. I should have been in tune with them. I'd have been able to stop it.

But no, I wouldn't, because I had no idea what was causing them to shift like they were, out of control and in agony. My bite had to be a catalyst of some sort. And I couldn't take that back.

Please. I tapped into my beast mind, hoping for an answer. Instead, I sensed a wall and a stubborn nagging feeling that I already knew what needed to be done.

"Cal, what's happening?" Kane stared out of the window, and I followed his line of sight, making out Vancouver's skyline.

We were home. *Home.* My heart constricted, and I clenched my chest. I had to stay calm. My emotions would only make things worse for Johnny and Levi. *Deep breaths. Steady heart.*

"Fuck," Kane muttered. "Get him on a private jet. Cost is no barrier. Bring him here. There's nothing I can do for him while he's there." He ended the call then roughly jammed his fingers into his hair.

"Johnny's in Toronto, isn't he?" I knew he was. He was confused, angry, scared. His primal instincts surged through our connection. He wanted to be with me. He thought I was in danger because I was spiking him with worry. It was a vicious cycle of emotion, and I'd been so stupid not to realize it would be impacting him as well.

"He's fucked up like Levi." Kane cursed under this breath. "Can't hold his form."

"I'm sorry. This is my fault. My bite—"

Kane shifted his eyes to me, and my next words dried up. I gulped down the lump in my throat, but it wouldn't go away. I was choking on my fear, and that was only going to end up causing more problems for everyone.

Get a grip, Charlie. Levi and Johnny will feel your panic.

"We don't meddle with this shit for a reason." Kane's tone was bordering on fury as he spoke through clenched teeth.

"I thought..." But I didn't know what I thought, because at the time I was going on instinct.

Kane didn't bother to acknowledge my words. He was furiously texting, his brow pulled into a deep vee.

I was desperate to make this right. I just didn't know how.

"I need to check on Ruby," I muttered, not expecting Kane to respond.

I stumbled my way to the back cabin, not because the plane wasn't steady but because my pent-up frustration was pulsing against instinct to let my beast side out to take over and go primal. No matter how hard I pretended to be okay, I wasn't.

"You got me into this mess," I growled at myself. *Her* primal instincts. *Her* insatiable demands. I should never have agreed to meld her into my psyche. I should never have given into her needs. She forced me to bite them. She made it seem right. She should be in a cage. Locked up forever.

My stomach lurched at that thought, a traitor to myself.

She is me and I am her. We are one.

Act like it.

I leaned against the door to the back cabin, resting my exhaustion against the frame.

We'd given Ruby a healthy dose of werewolf level tranqs before we'd boarded the plane, and she was still asleep. She looked peaceful, despite the sheen of sweat on her face. Her eyelids fluttered restlessly, but that was the only indication that something was off.

I pushed away from the door then moved to the side of the bed. My fingers twitched, but instead of touching Ruby's face, I laid two fingers against her throat to check her pulse. It was still too high, too surgy. She might look like she was resting, but her body was revving, trying to prepare her for the change that was two moons away. I slid onto the bed next to her then took her hand, entwining my fingers with hers.

"I'm so sorry, Rubes." She couldn't hear me, I knew that, but she was in this situation because of me, and I needed her to know that I was going to do everything I could to help her.

Except, the only person who would know what to do was Levi, and he had his own issues to deal with.

Because of me.

I should have disappeared. As soon as I knew Sal had taken over the clan, I should have gotten on a plane and left Canada. I didn't need the money. I could have gone into hiding and none of this would have happened.

Ruby was going to die if we didn't find a way to ease her transition. The fact that she was going to become a werewolf was an afterthought. If she made it through to the other side, explaining to her that her life as she knew it was over would be heartbreaking. I wished I could cling to the delusion that she'd survive. She was strong, healthy and stubborn enough to make it through, but sometimes that wasn't enough. I'd seen bigger, meaner men fail to transition successfully.

The truth was that the bite mattered, and Ruby's had been a by-product of Andrew's, the bite of a transitioning human not the bite of a werewolf.

Selfishly, I wanted her to live...to be with me.

I should have wanted to ease her pain so she could die with dignity instead of what was coming for her. Either way, she was doomed. And she didn't ask for this. No sane human would.

Tears rolled down my cheeks. I wiped them away with my sleeve, but they wouldn't stop coming. I was weak—too soft to rule a clan, too messed up to lead anyone. How many people had to suffer because of my issues?

I should have remembered that when people got involved with me, they ended up dead. My mother. My father. Now Ruby. I couldn't let my mind wander to Levi and Johnny. That shit would tear me to pieces.

My phone buzzed. I sniffled, wiped my tears again then looked at the screen.

Bite her.

I blinked away new tears then brought my phone closer to my face as if that would change the message from Levi.

My phone rang, and I immediately accepted the call. "Levi, I'm sorry. I'm sorr—"

"You have to bite her," he rasped. "It's the only way to stabilize her."

"I can't!" My heart was in my throat, thudding like it wanted to escape. "That's insane!"

Ruby grimaced, no doubt reacting to my raised voice. Her eyes stayed closed, but her expression was pained.

"Look at what it's done to you," I tried to hush myself, but my words sound garbled. "Biting her will make things worse."

"No—" He groaned, his next words muffled.

"Levi!" I couldn't keep my voice down. Panic seized me like a chokehold. "Levi, what's happening? Answer me."

Kane appeared at the door, his chest heaving. "What's going on?"

"Charlie," Levi rasped, his voice raw. "You…have… to…mark…her."

I couldn't believe what he was saying. Yet at the same time, every beastly instinct inside became alert. My beast craved this. *Yes. Do it.*

"The bite balances everything. It's...the...only —" He screamed, wrenching my heart back down to my chest.

"Levi!" I dropped the phone as my hand shifted into beast mode, my body contorting, fangs dropping, my beastly awareness surging into my head, demanding we fix this. The primal need was relentless, urging me forward, the same primal need that had caused me to bite my uncle. The same one that had coaxed me into mating with Levi and Johnny.

Kane had my phone, and he was shouting at Levi, trying to get him to respond, but I was too busy fighting for control as my beast side switched my brain from logic to instinct. I reeled back, fighting against this urge to bite yet again.

My body turned toward Ruby like I had no control, and I was horrified, not knowing if my next actions would end my friend's life right here, right now. The only drive I had, clear as anything, was to bite.

No! I clawed at the threads that bound my beast and I together, pleading with that side of myself to be reasonable, to be calm. We couldn't murder the only friend I'd ever had.

My eyes rolled back, a wave of dizziness turning my vision foggy, and, in my mind, I saw...

A battle raging, werewolves fighting side by side, a female werebeast roared, her snout in the air, jaw wide, baring teeth, chest flexed, arms bulging. The answering call wrapped itself around my head, echoing with familiarity. As I blinked away the fog, I saw the threads of their connections. She pulsed her strength through those threads, out to each of her pack, amping them both physically and emotionally. I saw the connection as it coursed through the lines that bound them, and I saw when those pulses bounced back, racing toward her so she could absorb their answering calls.

I blinked to reality as my body surged forward, inches away from Ruby. Kane roared. He wrapped his arms around my bulky waist, attempting to hold me back.

But he was no match against the desires of my beast.

Confused, I continued to fight, trying to hold myself back but slowly, inch by inch, like I was moving through molasses, I finally got close enough to Ruby to do some damage. I elbowed Kane back, sending him flying to the wall with a sickening crunch. The plane teetered sideways.

The thundering approach of his men came toward the back room.

My monstrous arm swooped toward my friend, but instead of raking her down the middle, I surprised myself by taking her gently, reverently into my arms. Confused, I gave up the fight. Unhindered by my own objections, a new understanding washed over me.

I tenderly brushed away Ruby's hair, clumsy with my big fingers. I cleared her throat and bared her flesh, then without any hesitation, I lowered my gnarled muzzle to Ruby's neck and pierced her swiftly.

Ruby didn't cry out, but her mouth opened, along with her eyes, wild with panic at first, only to calm as my bite penetrated her awareness. The link between us snapped into place instantly and, as I pulled myself back, sliding unconsciously to my human form, I knew what I had to do.

"Charlie?" Ruby croaked. "Did you…bite me?"

I caressed her cheek, and as I stared into her eyes, I sent all my love, my strength, my calm through our newly forming link. My mark spread along her skin, not a starburst like what Johnny and Levi had but spirals that moved from my bite toward her heart.

With every intention comes a mark. Words from the scripts that Kane had read out loud to all of us. *With every mark comes a bond. With every bond comes a commitment.*

"You're safe. You're going to be fine." I kissed her forehead, and as our connection snapped firmly into place, her trust and love rebounded back to me. "Rest, friend." I sent the command through our tether, and Ruby closed her eyes.

It was more power than I could fathom, but my beast felt perfectly at home with it.

I rubbed my hand over my face and the cobwebs cleared from my thoughts. I'd always known what to do. I only had to accept it.

"What have you done?" Kane roared as he pulled me roughly away from Ruby.

I let him tear me off the bed. I didn't fight when he shook me like a rag doll. When he hauled me up his body and gripped my face, glaring daggers into my soul, I let him do that too.

"Answer me, Charlotte."

"I saved her." I met his glare with confidence settling my feet to the floor, then rising up until I met him eye to eye, a little beastly reinforcement lengthening my spine. "And I know how to save Johnny and Levi, too."

Chapter Twenty-Four

Charlie

Once we arrived at the mansion, we got Ruby set up in a medical room where she would be contained while we waited to see how my bite impacted her transformation. For now, she was unconscious and resting, and I wasn't sure if it was because of the tranqs or because of my bite. Either way, I was grateful for the reprieve. She was here, with me, and I'd be able to guide her through the worst of it. I mean, that's what I thought would happen. I was going on beastly instinct. No more cutting people off from my thoughts, my emotions. From now on, I'd be open to them, including my pack and my mates...and now Ruby.

I turned my attention to the werewolves who needed me most. Johnny was on the way via the fastest jet Duke money could buy. He'd land in a couple of hours, which gave me time to focus on my other suffering mate.

Levi hadn't greeted us when we arrived, and he wasn't answering his cell.

I knew where to find him, though.

"I'm going for a run."

"Is this part of your grand plan?" Kane's sarcasm was unwelcomed, but he didn't relent. "Stretch your legs before you save the day?"

"Just keep an eye on Ruby," I said over my shoulder. "I'll be back soon."

I could tell he was bristling at my command, but I ignored his glare and shut down any further argument by shifting to my wolf. His attitude made me wonder if he was really all about giving up leadership to me or if that was his code for me being a figurehead in name only while he ran the pack from the sidelines. There'd be some ego busting happening if that were the case.

If I was to become queen, he'd have to get used to taking orders—at least outside of the bedroom.

Something to tackle later.

The automatic doors at the back of the main hall swooshed open, and I bolted into the lush grass of the expansive yard, set on tracking Levi down in the forest.

The air was ripe, heady with moss and turned-up earth, and the scent of wolf was sharp in my muzzle. He was shedding aggression mixed with confusion, leaving an unmistakable trail for me to track him. I knew it was on purpose. He wanted me to find him. The pulse along our connection was full of need. Even though I was sending a call out to him to stay calm, I knew he wasn't getting it fully. Our thread wasn't a two-way street—not completely, not yet anyway and I needed it to be.

I skirted along the perimeter of the forest, head down, focused on finding an entry point that would hide my approach. The leaves rustled in the breeze, and the smell of the sea stung my nose. I huffed, holding back a sneeze, then dove into the brush where a small tunnel gave me access to the undergrowth, keeping me disguised from Levi's keen senses.

I wanted to take him by surprise so I could watch him as he struggled for control. I needed to confirm my theory before I put my plan into action, and that could only be done if Levi thought he was alone. I toned down my homing beacon, muting my psychic caresses against his unconscious mind and limited my own echolocation ability to detect his essence then slinked through the undergrowth.

I didn't need wolf ears to know what direction to go. By the thrashing ahead, twigs snapping, leaves rustling, I knew I'd found him.

I slipped between two brushes, then partially shifted into semi-werebeast mode so I could leap, then scramble into a tree, cringing as my claws scraped and gouged through the bark.

Levi was below me, sprawled on the forest floor, his body mid-transition, twisted in a way that looked painful. His head was in wolf form, his muzzle digging into his side where his ribs stretched and expanded, pulling his flesh taut as the bones seemed to pop out of place then back again.

I could see the agony on his face as he arched back, his muzzle to the sky, jaw stretched beyond normal. I knew the pain that came from partial shifts, but my body was made to accommodate it. The male werewolf wasn't equipped to handle the muscle ripping, bone-jarring shifts.

He moaned a strangled sound as his body shifted back to human, and he collapsed into the forest dirt, panting, his body shaking with violent tremors.

Levi, I called to him through my thoughts, pulsing the thread that bound us. *Stop fighting the shift.*

He jolted, his eyes narrowed, then lifted his face and howled, his fangs dropping, claws sprouting, fur rolling over his body like his skin was tearing to shreds in order to make room for his wolf. He shuddered, his whole body vibrating as he fought to release his locked joints.

"Levi," I said out loud, crouching in the tree above him. "Let go."

He looked up, his eyes, dark pools of blue, filled with pain. He huffed through a few deep breaths, his teeth clenched, jaw locked in a grimace.

"Stop fighting," I said, pulsing the thread between us with intention. "Let your beast out." Because that's what my bite had ignited in him and, presumably, Johnny. I'd unleashed a beast version of both men similar to my own.

He groaned, fell back to the ground, his back arching so that he was on his heels and shoulders, his spine curved like a bridge. His abs were pulled so tight that I could see every twitch of his muscles as he screamed.

He reached clawed hands toward me. His jaw opened wider once again, fangs dropping past his chin. His body sprouted fur.

In this half-formed state, it was the closest he'd ever be to the werebeast form.

And it was what I needed from him to make my plan work.

I leapt from the tree to land at his side. His eyes flashed to me with frenzy. He raked his claws down my arm, opening rivulets, drawing a stream of blood. I held steady as I leaned into him, gritting my teeth and baring my throat.

"You know what to do." I pulsed him again with my intention. *Bite me.*

He froze, whimpered. He was fighting the urges I knew were surging through him. I leaned closer as I snaked my arms around his body, yanking him closer, forcing him to my throat.

"Bite me, Levi. Listen to your instincts!"

He howled, an eerie guttural sound, and the wash of his hot breath was the only warning I got before he sunk his fangs deep into my throat and marked me with his bite.

* * * *

Your fangs, the depth they pierced, sent tendrils into my body, anchoring us together as you took me to our place in my mind. Tumbling through the ether until we landed on a bed of shadows, your mouth sucked against my skin, softening the burn of your bite.

As you pulled away, dislodging your canines, a whoosh of pure lust flashed through me, igniting every nerve ending, pulsing against each erogenous zone.

Your eyes said 'possession' in the same way that my heart felt about you.

"Charlie," you said, lisping against your teeth, unused to speaking with longer fangs. Your eyes spoke a language all their own. You were excited. You were intrigued. You were in awe. "You've turned me into a beast."

I grinned, brushing my hand along your face, taking you in just as you were. "My beast."

"My queen," you said back to me, your caress against my breast, above my heart enough to tell me everything you were feeling as surely as the pulse of our new connection.

I slipped my fingers into your hair, tugging you down to me at the same time. When your lips crashed against mine, we came together like thunder and lightning.

You lashed me with your tongue, stroking my mouth like you were coaxing a fire. I devoured you right back, taking everything you gave me with a moan that you swallowed whole.

You gripped my body, cupping my breast, my hip, wedging your thigh between my legs so I was mad with the need to grind against your skin.

I held your ass, my fingers splayed to keep you in place as I tugged my fingers through your hair, nails scratching against your scalp. I made my way down your neck to the solid ridges of your shoulder.

You groaned against my lips when I snaked my hand around to play with your nipple, teasing and flicking, just as you were doing to mine.

When you slid down my body, you left a trail of lava. Your mouth was fire and my body gasoline. Every part of me that you touched, ignited and pleasure overwhelmed me.

When you latched onto my nipple, your fangs grazing against the sensitive skin, I cried out and thrust myself against your lips. You slipped your fingers into my pussy, your thumb against my clit and you sank your fangs into me once again.

My orgasm exploded, a bomb that your fangs detonated. My breast burned with a pleasure so pure that I couldn't help but whimper.

"Levi, I want you. I want all of you."

And you knew that the time was ripe for us to leave the shadow world and be one in real life.

Chapter Twenty-Five

Levi

The transition from Charlie's dreamworld to the real world was as seamless as my fangs gliding into the flesh of her breast, marking her again as my beastly instincts demanded. I was human once more, skin rather than fur, but I felt the power of my new identity.

Charlie made me her equal in physical strength, and now we were bonded in every way that mattered.

I wrapped my arms around her, cradling her waist and the back of her neck, rolling our bodies until I'd maneuvered us from top to bottom, shifting Charlie underneath me. She looked up through hooded eyes, her lashes fluttering seductively, then spread her legs to accommodate my hips. My cock pressed against her slick pussy, eager to penetrate her, just as my fangs had.

This was the moment I'd been dreaming about since Charlie had first called me to her. This moment had been fantasy fodder for three years.

My arms shook as I held myself back, staring down at her, marveling at what she'd given to me.

"Charlie, I —"

She tilted her face up, her lips ripe, glistening and red. I forgot what I wanted to say. No words would convey my feelings, anyway.

"I know, Levi," she said, her voice husky. She laid her hand against my chest, over my heart. "It's the same for me."

I pulled her closer, crushing our bodies together, taking her lips, kissing her as deeply as I thrust my dick, sinking into her cushion and dying a thousand deaths from the ecstasy of it all.

She wrapped her legs around my waist, her arms around my shoulders and together we devoured each other's lips. We rocked a rhythm all our own, and it felt so perfectly right that I wanted to freeze time and hold her there forever.

She arched into me, pressing her breasts against my chest, angling her hips so that each time I sank into her I was diving deeper, going harder. I gripped her ass then flipped her over, breaking from our kiss to watch her settle herself upright then ride my cock with all the control of a queen.

She rolled her hips and let her head fall back. Her tits perked up, and I couldn't help but cup them from below, teasing her peaked nipples with a forceful pinch that made her moan.

I wanted to close my eyes and get lost in the feel of her tight pussy wrapped around my cock but watching her glorious body move over me, grinding down hard enough to make my dick weep with pent-up cum was enough to keep my eyes pinned open.

She was sensual and wild, her fingers working her clit and her nipples as I clenched her ass and encouraged her to go faster, harder, more.

Looking up at her, seeing her glorious power as she rode me, filled my heart, my soul, my cock with blissful satisfaction.

I felt her orgasm take hold. Her legs shook as she relentlessly chased the high. My own climax crested, my balls tight to the point of pain, my cock a steel rod, but held back, urging her to take what she needed from me. As her climax exploded, her pussy spasmed, quivering, her body shaking, her moan long and guttural. I followed her, spewing my load and bellowing a release that made the night birds take flight all around us.

Chapter Twenty-Six

Kane

Cal and Revel carried Johnny between the two of them, dragging him by the shoulders as his unsteady feet attempted to keep the momentum going. He looked rough, but thankfully, he was still in one piece.

"He shifted a few times on the plane. Looks like he's in a lot of pain," Cal said as he leaned Johnny into the large lounge chair in my den. Johnny's head lolled, and his eyelids fluttered closed. I could keep an eye on him if he was passed out. He'd stay out of trouble for a little while at least.

"Where's Andrew?" I turned my attention to the door again.

"Right behind us." Revel stood sentry at the door, obviously expecting Johnny to jump up and make a run for it, which was always a wise course when it came to my brother.

Two of Johnny's guys who I'd never meant but knew existed, hauled Andrew in, one keeping a firm hold on the scruff of his neck. He'd obviously given up fighting and moved his feet on his own, but the look on his face was far from resigned.

"Put him there," I pointed to the chair in front of me as I leaned back against my desk, slightly probed up, arms folded.

Andrew hadn't been what I would call a formidable alpha. He'd never been imposing or batshit crazy like Sal, but there was always a cunning edge to his eyes that pulsed danger, if only as a threat to what *may* happen. There had been rumors, of course, about werewolves disappearing and lesser alpha's stepping away from their packs to make room for Andrew to swoop in and absorb them into his fold, but it was all vague, like a mythology about what might happen if Andrew pulled some of his many strings. He wasn't known as much for his might as he was for his strategy.

Which was why seeing him like this, physically defeated, was not an indication of his surrender. I knew behind his bloodshot eyes there was scheming going on.

"Let's set aside the pretense and get right to it. You hunted Charlotte in order to take her back to Sal." I stayed where I was, directly in front of Andrew, too close for him to get up without coming chest to chest with me.

"You're wrong." Andrew tried to keep the steel in his voice, but his conviction wavered when I growled my opinion about his words. "You may think I'm lying but I'm not. My intention was to get Charlie out of harm's way."

"By sending a knife-wielding thief to kidnap her?" I dropped my arms to clench my fingers around the edge of my desk.

"It had to look real." Andrew darted his eyes from me to the corner, and I saw him tense.

Johnny was rousing, mumbling and moaning. His men were just outside the door, within earshot and ready to deal with him. I appreciated their loyalty, not that I expected anything less from weres created by Johnny.

"Get him to his suite," I said with a nod to my brother's semi-prone form. "Don't let him out of your sight. Lex," I hollered, knowing he'd be within earshot. "Show them the way."

"Yes, sir," Lex's voice echoed. "Follow me."

Andrew tracked the other's movements, his body rigid. I kept my eyes on him, knowing he couldn't be trusted. I didn't think he'd be stupid enough to bolt, but fear could do a lot of things to a man, to a wolf, when he was cornered.

"We have no purpose for you other than what information you may have, so I suggest you get talking before I decide your information isn't worth your life." *Harsh but true.* Andrew was a liability at this point. Word would reach Sal sooner than later that we had his brother here. While I never sensed any diehard loyalty between the siblings, Sal would definitely want to get Andrew back into the fold rather than leave him here with us.

"You think you have it all figured out, don't you?" Andrew's eyes narrowed as he swung his gaze back to me. "You don't know what she's capable of."

"I know exactly"—I lunged forward, grabbing Andrew by his collar and yanking him close enough that I could see his nostrils quivering and the burst blood vessels in his eyes — "what she's capable of."

"I-I-I w-w-want to h-help." He stammered through another few words that were unintelligible. "Please." His hands were up in surrender, his eyes wide, body trembling. "S-she's m-my s-sister."

I eased off and let him sink back into the chair. "Stop dicking around."

"Charlie's special," Andrew said as he pulled at his collar, adjusting it back to normal. "There are stories… old tales that Dominic…that our father used to tell us."

"About Charlie?" I knew the stories he was talking about, but I wanted to see if he had a new take on it.

Andrew shook his head. "A-a-bout a powerful female alpha." He sucked in a deep breath and scrubbed his hand down his face. "Charlie always thought it was bullshit, but I knew there was truth there. Our father believed wholeheartedly. He used to tell me to protect her. Made me promise that if he died before he could position her, that I would need to get her away until the time was right."

"So, you're saying you ousted Charlie for her own good?" There had to be an ulterior motive, because no alpha would protect a woman who was destined to take his place. My body froze, my breath caught and I was stuck on that thought.

I *was* the kind of alpha who would protect the very female destined to take my place.

And yet…I wouldn't take her bite, even though I knew there were consequences she didn't foresee. Levi and Johnny were fucked up right now. But still, I didn't accept that she could bite me and make me hers.

I shook my head...hard, then pulled myself back from Andrew to pace a path around my desk, putting some distance between us.

"I had people watching her. But when Sal came back, I knew I had to act. I went to her myself. I staged a kidnapping to make it look believable because I knew Sal would be on to me and after Charlie."

I refocused on what Andrew was saying, forcing my own inner clusterfuck confusion to the back. I'd have to sort out my feelings, my self-imposed roadblocks about Charlie's bite later.

Andrew was leaving Gareth out of the equation completely. I decided to play along, see what kind of story he spun. "Sal insinuated that you were ousted."

"He would." Andrew snorted. "The truth is, he was working my men from the outside in. I didn't see it coming, not in its totality anyway. I had my eyes on...other things. When he came at me with his grand idea to take over his rightful place..." Andrew air-quoted the last two words... "I knew I had to get the hell out of there before I wound up dead like Dad."

"Are you saying your brother killed Dominic?" I stopped pacing to glare. If we had proof of that, we'd be able to wipe Sal off the planet for patricide, and no one would get in our way.

"Not by his hand and not that you could trace to him but yeah, I have a gut feeling it was the start of his plan to return to the pack." He speared me with a dark look. "I've been trying to dig up enough evidence to pin him with his crimes...all of his crimes, for the last three years, but he's too greasy for anything to stick."

"So, you're aware that Sal is hunting female werewolves?" I leaned on my desk, forcing my clenched knuckles to flatten.

"Everyone is aware of that." He sighed. "Which is why he wants Charlie."

"He had her, so why did he give her up?"

Andrew's skin grew pale, and he licked his lips. "Because he knows about your family prophecy and that you and your brothers are the catalysts to her full powers."

"What do you mean...catalysts?"

"I mean, for her to reach her full potential, she needs to not only take your bite, the bite of all three of you males, but to give one, too." Andrew licked his lips and tugged at his collar. "He believed coming here would ignite her instinct to rise to her full potential."

Dread pooled in my gut, a feeling of missing something vital in my plans settled deep in my bones.

"And what happens if the catalyst initiates?" My fists were clenched again, and I was fighting the impulse to leap over the desk and grab Andrew by the throat.

"I become all powerful...queen material," Charlie said at the door, her voice a grumble as it slid past her werebeast fangs.

Chapter Twenty-Seven

Charlie

Andrew hit the ground on his knees, his hands steepled like he was praying. "Charlie, I tried to help you. I was always on your side."

I wanted to bite him. I wanted to rip his throat out. Instead, I stood still, willing my werebeast urges to calm the fuck down and hold position. No matter how grotesquely pathetic this was, I couldn't act on my impulses.

Sensing my conflict, Levi pulsed strength through our connected threads, urging my rage to settle and simmer instead of explode.

"Levi, what the fuck?" Kane rushed toward us, taking a few steps before halting with a look of shock, anger and confusion mingled on his face. I knew Levi, who was just behind me, had morphed into beast mode. I knew he was trying to rein in his own instincts to lash out, not because he suddenly hated his brother, but he was surging with aggression, thanks to our shared bites. Part of me was in him and him in me. I ebbed some of the same calming essence back to him, completing a cycle of chill so we both wouldn't do something we'd regret.

I glanced over my shoulder and met his eyes. They were vividly blue, as always, but they held his usual Levi awareness. He nodded once, and I knew he had things under control.

"What did you do to him?" Kane roared.

Levi stood seven feet tall now and looked as beastly as I did, except he was more primal and hadn't yet mastered the ability to speak, so it was up to me to deal with his brother.

I stepped in Kane's way, ducking under the doorframe to fit into the room. "He's mine now." My words came out garbled, like I was speaking through a mouthful of rocks. I hadn't meant to say it that bluntly but there it was, Levi belonged to me and I to him.

Kane narrowed his eyes as he shifted his gaze past me and back to his brother. "You're a beast."

"We completed the loop. He has my bite, and I have his." I flexed my arms, the muscles tight like coils.

"Which means you're one-third of the way to Sal's ultimate plan." Andrew's voice still held a quiver, and he was on his knees, but he no longer looked quite as pathetic as he had moments before.

"Three bites?" I moved closer to him, towering, my fangs aching to take a bite. "What will three bites do for Sal? Other than bring him one step closer to his own destruction."

"Are you kidding?" Andrew balked. "Have you ever known Sal's ego to allow him a moment of thought when it comes to common sense?" He sat back on his heels. "He wants you to get all three bites so he can hunt and kill you. He says you'll be the ultimate prize."

I scoffed. Kane grumbled. Levi stepped closer to me, pulsing me with a surge of protective anger.

I reached behind me to touch his furry arm. Squeezing enough to tell him to stand down.

"He thinks he has it all figured out, and he has a bunch of messed up witches backing him." Andrew shook his head. "You'll be powerful, sure, but he'll have magic on his side and all the dirty tricks you won't see coming."

"Oh really?" I bulked up, taking up more space and sucking the air out of the room. "I don't think he really knows what I'm capable of."

Andrew gave me a once-over that made me want to kick him.

"Charlie, you're magnificent." Andrew cleared his throat. "Dad always said…" He waved his hand up and down. "But I didn't know until now what he meant. You're truly a queen."

"Shut up, Andy," I barked, ignoring his warning about Sal. I needed time to process the information. "You've fucked things up. You know your actions led to my best friend taking a feral's bite? Why'd you go after her boyfriend like that?"

Andrew's smile slid off his face. "He came at me with a pipe. I reacted. I wasn't trying to hurt your friend or her boyfriend. I was keeping watch."

I snorted, my arms crossed, knowing it must look comical for me to stand this way, but it wasn't like my human mannerisms disappeared when I was in beast mode.

"I'm telling you the truth. Here—" He rolled his head to the side. "If you don't trust my words, then mark me. I'm ready to bow a knee to your leadership."

I shook my head, gagging at the idea of taking on another werewolf who was a relative. Blood relation or not, having my uncle tied to me was already gross enough.

"Stand up and act like you have some respect for yourself," I growled.

Andy jumped to his feet, so eager to obey. It was suspicious, and I didn't trust him, but his offer to take my bite did give me an idea.

"You say that Sal wants me to get three bites? That's why he sold me to Kane?"

"He would have put something in the contract for purchase, too." Andy nodded, his Adam's apple bobbing as he swallowed. "Now that you have one, the other two will follow quickly. According to the scrolls, each bite brings a physiological change that calls to the others."

Kane took a step back from me like I was suddenly contagious.

I rolled my eyes.

Levi grunted.

"What scrolls?" I filled in for Levi.

"The ancient texts. We don't have the complete story, but we believe that you're *the* one—the beast destined to become the top wolf. When you get the three bites, you become the queen of the wolves. That's when Sal will put his plan into action."

"His plan to hunt me?" Things were starting to make sense to me. Sal's grand scheme to murder me would, of course, be attached to his ego.

"Charlie, I know you think he has no chance at killing you, but the scrolls say differently and so do the scholars. They've told Sal that he can beat you, and once he does, he'll bite you and absorb all your pack connections, all of your wolves' allegiance and loyalty, before he kills you. They'll all belong to him, and he'll be the most powerful alpha in Vancouver."

"That son of a bitch," Kane growled. "Why are the scholars pandering to him?"

I ignored Kane's venting, not because I wasn't equally as baffled by the scholars' actions but because I just couldn't handle one more thing. *Not right now.* "And Sal thinks he'll be able to kill me with his bite?" It was hard to believe that one simple bite could do so much damage, and yet, one bite had already changed my world drastically.

"He'll kill you however he can. He's got witches on his side, and he'll do you dirty. Let me join you. I'll be your right hand." Andrew was groveling again, his eyes pleading.

"I already have my right hand," I said and felt Levi puff his chest out behind me. "But I agree, we need you with us and under the control of my pack. I want the scrolls Sal has, and you're going to get them for me."

"I can't go after the scrolls... That's a death sentence... A lone wolf —"

"Oh, you won't be alone." I leaned forward, glaring. "You'll be working with one of my lieutenants... Gareth."

Andy flinched. His face drained of all color. His shoulders sagged.

"Oh, you didn't realize I already know about your little alliance with my uncle?"

"I needed help to get out of Vancouver! Gareth wanted to—"

"He wanted to capture me!" I roared. "To force his bite on me. Don't tell me you're that stupid, Andy. You knew what he wanted from me!"

Andy lowered his head and let out a sob. "I thought I could outsmart him." He held his hands up and out, begging once again.

It was revolting.

"You've only ever looked out for yourself, Andy. You've only ever done what would benefit you."

His shoulders shook. His eyes were damp. I wanted to rip his throat out.

"You weren't trying to save me. You were trying to capture me, just like the rest of them." I crouched low enough so I could snort in his ear, and my fang tips touched his jaw. "Just like the rest of them, you underestimated me."

I stepped out of Levi's way, pulling back from Andrew before I did something irreversible. Levi was huffing and puffing, his body pent-up, full of intention.

"You know what to do," I said.

Levi didn't give Andrew a chance to react. He was on him in a second, piercing into his throat, ravaging the skin right down to his esophagus. Andrew's scream was cut short, blood poured from his mouth. Levi sank his fangs deeply into Andrew's flesh to mark my stepbrother as his own minion, then he dragged Andrew from the room—a beast carrying his prize.

Kane looked ready to pounce or maybe to run. Either would have been unsurprising. I turned slowly to him, my chest heaving as I strained to maintain control. Blood was blood, and my beastly instincts craved more. "Are you ready to see this through now?"

"No." Kane tore his eyes from the empty doorway then took another step away from me. "I'm not. This is happening too fast. We need time to strategize. If you take my bite, then all that's left is Johnny, and we can't ignite Sal's plan before we're ready for him."

He's holding back? After everything we'd learned? He still didn't understand. "We can strategize after I've reached full power."

"No. Charlie, you aren't thinking this through. We need a plan." Kane walked around his desk, putting it between us.

"I have a plan. Sal wants me, so that's what he'll get—me in my full glory." I pounded my chest. "He won't beat me like this."

"You're drunk on power, Charlie," Kane growled, his hands splayed on his desk as he leaned forward to glare at me. "We don't know what Sal has in his arsenal. That collar his witches created was no joke. You felt it. You know. I wouldn't put it past him to have a lot of other devious plans in the works."

My mind flickered to that day, the burn of the collar and how it took me out instantaneously. I lifted a gnarled furry hand to touch my throat. I could still feel the pain like an angry ghost against my skin. The memory tamped my bloodlust down like cold water on a fire.

"Are you really willing to take a chance without knowing? To sacrifice the men who will be linked to you if you take my bite?" Kane moved closer. "It could be their death sentence, along with yours."

His words hit like punches. I shuddered and, as I did, my body shifted to human, unbidden and uncontrolled. I went from seven feet to five. It changed my perspective instantly.

177

He was right. *Fuck.* I couldn't run into this without a solid plan. I couldn't put the pack at risk because of my reckless decisions.

"Sal had the contract amended." My mind, already steps ahead of me, lingered on that day, just before I was collared when I was in the elevator. Andrew's words, *"he would have put something in the contract for purchase, too,"* took on new meaning.

Kane frowned. "The contract for you?" He had the sense to look ashamed.

That day should never have happened.

"I overheard his lawyers talking about the contract. That he needed an amendment added." Conclusions were forming, their conversation making my shoulders bunch and a chill trail over my skin.

"There wasn't anything new on the contract. I reread it before I signed." Kane swore as his eyes darkened. "Unless it was added in witch text."

"Like a spell?" I'd heard of witches using spell work to add lines of text to binding contracts, small print that was only visible if you were looking for it. "That fucking bastard!"

"I should have had Levi with me." Kane's shoulders dropped. "He would have known something was wrong with the paperwork."

The enormity of what this meant hit me hard. Fury lashed me, and I wanted to howl, to scream, to rip Kane's office apart. If these men hadn't meddled in my life, none of this mess would have happened.

Kane turned his back to me, shutting me out if only because he knew he fucked up.

Always shutting me out!

"We need to find out what you agreed to," I growled.

Kane nodded, running his hand through his hair so it spiked haphazardly. "I'm sorry, Charlie." His voice sounded defeated, and it hit me, a sucker-punch to the gut.

I breathed through my anger. I tamped down my instinct to lash out with words. I might not have asked for this. I might not have invited the chaos, but I did make the first move. I called these men into my life before they knew what baggage I brought with me. Sure, it was unconscious. Sure, it was unintentionally real, but I couldn't blame anyone else for that part.

The truth was, I wanted these men in my life, no matter what their choices had done to me.

"What's the plan, then?" I tempered my tone and stepped to him, bypassing the desk so I could brush my fingers along his.

He turned his hand so he could entwin it with mine, a gesture that was heart melting and spoke to his state of mind. He blamed himself for it all. With his head still bowed, he sighed. "I don't have one."

"Yet," I said as I tugged his hand so he turned.

He looked down at me, sorrow, maybe regret, etched on his face. I offered a tiny smile.

Kane raked his hand over his face. "Yet."

"We're in this together." I leaned in, rose on tiptoes, tenderly brushed my lips against his before pulling back. "With or without a bite." Mistakes were made but if I was supposed to be a queen, I'd need to be the bigger person and figure out a way to make it right.

Shouting sounded from the hall. Claws clacking on marble. Boots hitting closely behind.

I turned just in time to see Johnny in wolf form, diving toward me. His body hit full force and he took me down hard, ripping my hand from Kane's as we slid across the floor of the den, bunching up the rug that spanned the room. His paws were on my shoulders. His mouth was wide, his fangs gleaming. His eyes were liquid silver.

He lifted his head then howled, and as he did, he shifted to human form.

"Johnny, we can't do this." Even though I wanted him to. "We have to wait." There was no conviction in my words. They were hollow, just like my willpower. "You don't understand."

Yet, I wanted what he was offering.

I turned my head, exposing my throat to his fangs. This was what I needed. One more bite.

"Do it," I urged.

Johnny nuzzled my throat, his fangs scraping against my skin.

"Johnny, no!" Kane roared, his thundering footsteps pounding toward us.

Chapter Twenty-Eight

Johnny

It was too late.

Charlie was mine.

Kane be damned.

My fangs retreated into my gums, a strange feeling while in human form, partial shifting was never something I'd experienced before Charlie's bite.

Charlie wasn't bleeding but she was covered in blood, and I had the most intense need to care for her.

"Johnny...what have you done?" Kane didn't step any closer as I pulled Charlie into my arms and against my chest. She wasn't dead, far from it. I felt the surge of our bond locked into place between us. She was floating in her dream world, where I wanted to join her, but not here, not yet.

"I followed my instincts," I said as I stood, matching Kane's height as I always did but holding more authority than him now. With the bond in place, I outranked him as far as I was concerned. Charlie had chosen me. She'd chosen Levi. We'd joined her.

Kane had made another choice, which meant he was on the outside.

"You've put her in more danger than you understand," Kane roared, spit flying, eyes sparking fire. "You're playing right into Sal's game with your lack of control."

He lunged as if to take Charlie from me, his fangs poking just under his lip.

I took a step back, startled by his rage. I'd seen him unleash fury before, but this was something else.

Jealousy?

No. Something deeper.

Loss.

"Stay away from us until you calm down, brother." I turned my back on him then walked out of the den. Behind me, I heard him pound against his desk, no doubt splintering some part of it by the sound of the loud crack and groan. Glass shattered next.

He roared so loud the walls shook, but I kept going and Charlie kept sleeping. It was my duty to protect her, to care for her.

I brought her to my wing of the mansion, my men standing sentry at the double doors. "No one gets in without my permission. Do whatever is necessary to give us privacy."

Keith nodded once as he closed the doors behind us.

"Charlie, baby," I whispered against her ear as I laid her down on the leather couch. "Come back to me." I felt my desire to have her awake like a jolt leaving my body and just as quickly as it left, Charlie opened her sleepy eyes.

"I was having the best dream about you," she purred, her lips curled into a seductive smile.

"Well, how about we bring it into the real world?" I started to help her sit up but she was like a spring and captured my face between her palms.

"Johnny, I feel you inside me now." She kissed me softly and my body, already primed with need, took over my thoughts.

I slipped one hand around her waist and one into her hair, tilted her head, then kissed her properly. She opened to me, darting her tongue against mine, pushing her body forward so she wrapped her legs around my waist and her hot heat was pressed into my groin.

I would never get enough of her taste, the feel of her body against mine, tits crushed to my chest, hands wrapped around my shoulders, legs tightly clenched and pussy so snug that I wished with everything I had that we were naked.

The tang of blood, metallic and sharp reminded me of my goal to get her cleaned up but with an improvised mission now.

I lifted her with ease, carrying her while devouring her mouth, holding her up by her ass and taking her straight into my bathroom.

Sensing the change in venue, Charlie launched herself away from me so abruptly that I felt the urge to chase her, but she was only a few feet away, a sparkle in her eyes, understanding and intent clear.

"We've never done this in my dreams," Charlie said, a sly grin on her puffy pink lips.

I somehow had sense enough to turn the shower heads on by the master control at the door, four waterfalls jetting from the walls, two overhead sprinklers raining hot steamy water down from the ceiling. We stood just outside of our ultimate destination staring at one another.

"You go first," Charlie said with a seductive sweep of my body. "I want to see you for real."

She'd seen me and I'd seen her, naked as anything, many times in her shadow world, but I felt what she was feeling. This was different.

There was no way I'd tease her with taking it slow. My cock was straining so hard against my pants that I thought it might carve its way out before I even got my zipper down.

Charlie licked her lips, and my dick nearly exploded. I dropped my pants, steamy air hitting my balls and making my cock bob then ripped my shirt over my head. I flung it into the corner along with my pants then stood there while she appraised me, desperate for her to strip down, too.

But she was going to be a tease.

She circled me like a predator, her eyes trailing heat as she moved. Her breathing was ragged, even though she was trying to hide it.

"You're everything I dreamed, Johnny," she said, her voice holding a lilt of laughter. "And so much more in real life."

We both knew that what happened in her shadow world was just as real as what would happen out here, but that didn't change the fact that I wanted so badly to touch her for real, not floating in a world of her mind's creation.

I grunted when she lightly trailed her fingers along the muscles of my back. She came around to face me, moving two fingers up and over my shoulder, down my chest to circle my nipple. My cock wept pre-cum but I didn't make the first move.

She grinned, pulled her hand away, then took a step back.

Like a magnet drawn to metal, I followed her, taking a step in her direction, only for her to raise her finger again then wag it at me. "Nah-uh, eyes only."

She stood just outside the shower, steam billowing around her like she was a goddess.

My eyes were glued to her, waiting, hardly breathing, my dick hard, my balls tight.

She hooked her thumbs to the waistband of her shorts then slowly began to wiggle them over her hips, giving me a glimpse of tanned, plush skin I'd only ever seen in her dreams. I licked my lips. She slid her shorts down farther, revealing that she wore no panties, something I'd suspected but could only fantasize about. I clenched then unclenched my fists, pumping my fingers tightly to keep myself from ripping her clothes off myself.

She turned her back to me as she slipped her shorts down farther, her ass on display. My mouth watered, my heart thundered and I growled. "Woman, you're going to murder me with that ass."

A saucy grin over her shoulder was enough to kill me. She whipped up, her tank top coming off in one smooth sweep, followed closely by her bra, both landing on my cock, her bra dangling for a half a second of torture before I tossed it off then went for her.

She was laughing as she ran into the shower, already turning to embrace me as I rammed into her, taking her up in my arms and crushing my body against hers.

She moaned when I kissed her, thrusting my tongue deep, my hands on her ass, lifting her so her back was pressed against the shower wall.

"Johnny," she moaned.

I kissed along her jaw, down her throat, over the mark of my bite, pride wrapping itself around my heart. She wrapped her legs over my hips, hooking her ankles at my back, yanking me so close that my dick nestled against her pussy.

"Don't make me wait." She yanked my head up, meeting my eyes with determination. "Fuck me, Johnny."

There was no way I'd deny her now. I took her lips as I drilled her pussy, pushing my way into her sweet cushion.

"Yes!" she raked her nails down my back, spurring me to go deeper, harder.

There was no way this would last long — not the first round, anyway.

I'd waited too long.

And it seemed that Charlie had the same problem.

Her pussy quivered against my cock, squeezing as her orgasm rose, coaxing mine to creep like wildfire into my balls, along my shaft. I bellowed my release, spewing cum into Charlie like I was marking her.

She arched into me, her legs shaking, her pussy spasming, taking my thrusts with small grunts that drove me wild.

"Johnny," she sighed, "I want more."

I let her legs down slowly, holding her up against my body. "Your wish is my command, my queen."

Chapter Twenty-Nine

You came to me with fury and fire.

You came to me with sorrow.

You came to me with a look in your eyes that crushed my soul.

"I want you, Charlie, more than I can bear," you say, your mouth full of fangs, your instincts battling for purchase, torment swirling the amber of your eyes. "This isn't the way it's supposed to happen."

I wished you'd be more like your aggressive self right now. I wished you'd rail and beat your chest. I wished you'd threaten to punish me with your hands, your mouth, your body.

I wished you'd take what was yours.

Instead, you had regret in your eyes and poison on your tongue.

"I have to go. I have to find the truth before we do something irreversible."

You plead with me to let it be...to let you go. Not with your words but with your body. Keeping me at a distance with the tension that rolled off you, a hazy heat surrounding your body.

"Kane, no, you don't understand." I lunged for you, my arms outstretched, desperate to get closer, but the shadows swirled around me, keeping me from touching you. Like I needed protection from you. "This is the way. The right way. You don't understand because you don't feel it yet, but you will." I motioned him to move closer. "Take my bite, and you will."

I knew I sounded like a temptress, luring Kane to his doom, and I knew that he felt my siren call like a pull he didn't want to battle. His big body swayed toward me. I could just, with another inch, touch his skin with my outstretched fingers.

"No. Not yet." Kane pulled himself back with strength I knew cost him peace. "I have to find the truth, and you have to let me go." He lowered his eyes, his shoulders slumped. "You have to let me see this through my way, Charlie. You have to let me go."

Before I could form the words, the protest sitting heavy on my tongue, you came at me, fangs bared and fists clenched. "You have to let me go!" you roared, searing me with your anger.

The shadows pulled me back, sucking me away from your rage and the lava spewing from your eyes. But it was you, Kane, not a threat...not a monster.

As if to contradict my thoughts, your eyes sparked danger, and your fangs grew longer.

"And don't..." You ripped through the ether, somehow getting to me, despite the protections my world was making. You grabbed me by the back of my neck, hauling me closer, your anger so vivid that I wanted to close my eyes and wish myself awake.

This wasn't you...not the Kane I'd come to know.

"Don't you dare come looking for me."

Chapter Thirty

Charlie

I woke up with an ache between my legs and in my heart. Kane was gone. I knew by the silence all around me, his presence a physical feeling in the mansion that I'd never realized I'd miss until now.

I wanted to sob.

I wanted to scream.

I didn't have enough time with Kane. I felt like he was acting rashly, impulsively.

Running from me and what the prophecy said. A prophecy that he believed in.

A pulse of warmth ebbed through my connections to Levi and Johnny. Their souls were consoling me, trying to repair the damage that Kane had done. We were bonded on a level that I didn't understand but that felt like a warm hug.

Johnny's arm was thrown over my body, pinning me to the mattress. He was sound asleep, snoring lightly. It was totally cool that our bond would work even when he was unconscious. I couldn't help but laugh a bit. Of course Johnny would be capable of so much support, even just lying there. His glorious body, naked with his ass to the sky, candy to my roving eyes, was the best view to wake up to. That alone was enough to distract me from my angry, sad, what-the-fuck thoughts of Kane.

We'd fucked all night, into the early morning hours until my dreams had claimed me, and Kane had torn my heart out.

Now I lay there, back in my head, not really knowing what to do. Kane had left. He was gone. I wanted to chase after him, but his command to stay put had me debating against my own impulsiveness. I knew what my beastly instinct said—find him, bite him, complete the circle. But maybe he was right. Maybe my instincts were the problem. I listened to his concerns on the jet. I'd listened, but had I heard him? He wanted tradition. He wanted what he believed the legacy demanded.

The three-bite thing had taken this whole situation to another level. Complicated was now the name of the game.

"What's wrong?" Johnny's sleepy voice pulled me from my thoughts, his power of distraction once again saving me from myself. He tightened his hold on me then kissed my shoulder. I wanted to sink into him, to lose myself in his touch.

"Kane—" I choked on my next words.

Johnny sat up, shaking off sleep and coming to life in an instant. "He's gone." His hair was a mess of tangled knots dropping down his back, almost reaching his ass. The cut of his muscles, the vee down his back, the dimples just above his ass, made my body stir like we hadn't banged all night.

There was a knock at the door before either of us could do or say anything more. "Johnny, Charlie, get dressed. We need to talk." Levi's voice was resigned. He must have known that Kane was gone, and I hoped to fuck that he had a plan.

Twenty minutes later, Johnny had his hair under control and clothes on, which was sad but for the best. I needed to keep my head in the game, but being in the presence of both of *my* men had my body hot and definitely bothered.

"I've been going through the documents that were sent here after Kane—"

"Paid in full for me?" While I better understood the situation and why Kane felt he had no choice but to bid on me, a thought that still made me spark rage, I didn't get why he hadn't had a plan for duplicity. It wasn't like Sal was an unknown entity. The guy was dirty as hell. Kane should have anticipated something shitty going down, aside from buying a female werewolf. I'd be having nightmares about that collar for a long time to come.

"Yes, that," Levi said with shame in his voice and a pulse through our bond. "This contract has residual magic but nothing that screams witch text."

I marveled at Levi's ability to detect magic with a sense that no other wolf I'd known possessed. Even my beastly instincts, which could alert me with a feeling of doom or danger nearby, couldn't pinpoint magic with the kind of accuracy that Levi could.

"What I think happened was that Kane signed a multi-layered contract." He shifted some papers underneath the contract he held. "Like this." He ran his hand over the top. "The witch text could have been embedded in the carbon copies, but this top copy would have held only binding magic to ensure that the signature went through to the other sheets below. Standard practice for contracts these days and nothing Kane would have detected as being off."

"But you would have," I said as I reached for the top layer. The static charge that vibrated against my fingers was exactly what I'd expect from a contract constructed by witches. It would have alerted me, but I would have been suspicious of anything that came from Sal. I wasn't faulting Kane for not second-guessing, not really. He had a plan, however flawed. He just didn't truly understand how diabolical my stepbrother really was.

"I believe I would have, but this kind of magic is meant to hijack and gaslight." Levi sighed. "What's done is done, and we all feel horrible for what Sal did to you. I'm not minimizing it." He pulsed me again through our bond, and I reached out to squeeze his hand. "What we need now are the actual documents."

"Andrew and Gareth?" I knew they'd been sent on their mission, given direction from Levi while I'd been...preoccupied with Johnny.

"They've gone after the scrolls," Levi confirmed. "Andrew said they were housed in a vault at headquarters."

"Makes sense." I knew that to be where my father had kept some of the more sensitive or in need of protection items he'd possessed. I'd only ever been in the vault a handful of times, and I knew there were two ways in and out—one that was obvious and one that was hidden. "He'll know how to get them without detection."

"He checked Sal's office. No contract." Levi ran his hand through his hair.

"Could it be at the home office?" Johnny asked.

But that didn't fit. My father never kept anything important in the vault at home, too obvious. No, he'd have filed it with his right-hand man, who at the time was Carter. Now it was Vincent. Sal's guy. "It's with the accountant."

"The money man?" Levi frowned.

"He's not the regular kind of accountant. Vincent doesn't just manage the money. He manages everything related to the business, including holding documents like this one. He's a bulldog with a bite." I wasn't scared of him, but I knew to take heed and approach with caution.

"So we need to go after that guy." Johnny's bloodlust was a jolt to my senses, sent through our new bond like a shot of adrenaline.

It hyped me up. Taking a bite out of Vincent was suddenly my top priority. "I'm ready to take him down." Fuck caution. I wanted blood.

"If we go after one of Sal's top wolves, we'll be declaring war." Levi, the buzzkill, injected rational thinking with a smooth tone and calm ebb to coat Johnny's energy. "We can't do that without Kane around."

Effectively subdued and now fully frustrated, I snapped. "Are we going to talk about the fact that Kane is gone?" Even saying his name made me want to chase after him. It was an impulse, a yearning, and I knew with certainty that meant the three-bite theory was a thing—which also meant, I knew in my heart that Kane had to leave but I wouldn't say that out loud. "He fucking took off," I said, instead sounding like a jilted girlfriend.

"We talked," Levi said, maintaining his calm, no hard edges to his voice at all. "He's protecting the pack." He stared into my soul. "He left to protect you, us. You know that, Charlie."

Shame made my cheeks heat, and I looked at the floor. "Do you know where he's gone?" I needed to know like a compulsion driving me for information, any information, about Kane's whereabouts.

Levi's silence told me what I needed to know. He knew exactly where Kane had taken off to.

"Andrew told you about the three-bite theory?" Levi asked.

I nodded, meeting his eyes once again.

"What three-bite theory?" Johnny said. "Why'd Kane tell you where he was going and not me?"

We both looked at Johnny, realizing that we hadn't filled him in on anything since he'd bit me.

"I mean..." Johnny shrugged. "I guess I've been preoccupied," he said sheepishly.

"There's something in the scrolls that Sal has, ones we don't have, that says Charlie needs three bites, reciprocal bites, to reach her full power." Levi walked to the table with our scrolls spread out. "And each bite makes it harder for the chosen males to stay away."

"And Kane ran away because of that?" Johnny shook his head. "What the actual fuck? Since when does Kane run from danger?"

"Not that simple," Levi said as he shuffled the scrolls we had. "He left to buy us time. We need more information before we can proceed safely. He took off to avoid the pull...you know, the one that had you tackling Charlie in the den, in full out beast mode last night?"

Johnny's eyes went wide and his cheeks turned ruddy. "Okay, that shit was intense. Don't tell me you had it under control."

"I didn't take Charlie out like a maniac."

"It's my fault, really," I said, pulling both men away from their rising anger toward each other to me. "I should have had some restraint before I bit you both. I acted on instinct, but that doesn't mean I did the right thing."

Johnny closed the distance between us in two steps then swept me up into his arms. "You did the right thing by me." His height forced me to tilt my head way back just to look into his eyes. "I wouldn't change anything that happened."

"Neither would I, but you get what Charlie's saying," Levi said with a huff.

"I don't live with regrets, never have." *Or at least, I try not to.* I pushed Johnny back gently, disentangling myself from his embrace. "But some caution would have avoided where we are now."

Johnny threw his arms up. "Kane took off to delay the third bite, which means Charlie can't reach her full power." He looked from me to Levi. "And Charlie reaching her full power is bad?"

"It's what Sal wants. He's got something written in the contract that will ignite as soon as she gets and gives that third bite." Levi picked up the contract copy we had. "At least that's what we think. We won't know until we get the original."

"And we think Vincent Del Marr has the copy we want," I said. "So we need to get it without starting a war."

"Vincent Del Marr is Sal's accountant?" A wicked smile broke on Johnny's face. "Why didn't you say so? I know exactly how we'll do this."

Chapter Thirty-One

Johnny

Vincent wasn't someone I knew personally, but I did know his nephew well, so well in fact that I'd consider him a brother — a pack brother, to be exact.

"Hey, Lex, thanks for doing this, man." We'd met Lex outside of Vincent's side gig, an underground werewolf fighting ring that catered to humans' insatiable need for gambling. They thought they were betting on wolf dogs when the reality was much more sinister.

"No need to thank me, Johnny." Lex had his own trauma linked to this place, and I didn't blame him for the nervous twitch he had on his face. "If this is a way to put my uncle out of business, I'm in."

"That's the plan." *Eventually at least.* Lex knew we were after his uncle's allegiance. We all knew the guy was greedy as fuck and not really one of the most loyal werewolves out there. "You tell him what I told you to?"

"Yeah, I did." Lex shook his head. "He thinks this is about Kane taking off."

It was a calculated risk to let Vincent think that I was coming with a chip on my shoulder because what we told him was that Kane had left the pack. We all knew that if Vincent smelled blood, he'd want a taste.

He'd agreed to the meeting within minutes of Lex texting him from the club with an invite to his private estate.

"You'll stay out here until I signal?" I knew Charlie was itching to rip a strip off of Vincent. "No impulsive shit until I'm ready, okay?" I sounded like Kane, and Charlie gave me a fuck off and die expression. "Sorry. I'm just worried."

We were sitting in Lex's SUV, Charlie and Levi in the backseat, hidden by blackout windows.

"Don't worry about me, Johnny," Charlie said, no snark in her tone, as she reached forward, across the console to touch my arm. "I'll wait for your signal."

I started to turn, satisfied that Charlie would let me handle things to start.

"Unless you take too damn long," she said, teasing me.

"I can be fast as fuck." I flashed her a grin. "You know that."

She swatted me, and I trapped her hand before bringing her fingers to my lips. No words necessary. Her gaze softened, and warmth pulsed through our bond.

"See you soon," I said then exited the SUV.

Lex was a few steps ahead. "He has humans on the gate, some of Sal's minions, but inside there's a half dozen guys who are under his command."

"Sal allows his goons to have their own crew?" I might have acted like Kane had no idea about my own team, but my guys had been in and out of pack missions for years, my own right-hand men, and Kane had let it slide. Normally, it was taboo to bite alliance outside of the clan without express permission from the alpha.

"Vince does what he wants, always has. Besides, Sal won't say shit to him about having his own pack. He's been with Sal for a decade. Vince took him in when Sal was ousted."

That, I hadn't known.

"So, there's loyalty on both sides."

"As long as it's advantageous for Vince, sure. Loyalty is one word for it." Lex shook his head.

"Any last words of advice?" I knew I had the element of surprise. Vince had no idea I could go into beast mode now, but that didn't mean a dozen silver bullets wouldn't take me down.

"Yeah, don't piss him off."

We stopped at the security gate, having walked a half block up the street from where we'd parked. It wasn't the kind of arrival I was used to, but Vince wouldn't be paying attention to how we got there, and there was nowhere else to stash Charlie and Levi but in the SUV.

"Names?" A blond burly and bearded guy barely looked up from his computer. He had no visible weapons, but it didn't mean he wasn't armed.

"You know who we are, Teddy. Stop being a prick." Lex reached past the window opening to smack the guy upside the back of the head.

Teddy grunted but still didn't look up from his computer. "Fuck, dude, you almost screwed up my mission."

I craned my neck to see his screen. "What level are you on? You make it to the three-headed witch yet?"

That got Teddy's attention. "Fuck no! Shit!"

"She's tough but not unbeatable. Use your shield as a weapon. It's got something in it that she's allergic to."

"Thanks, man." Teddy flicked a button and the gates slowly started to open. "Where's your car this time, Lex? Roll it into a ravine?"

"Yeah, something like that." Lex reached past the window to swat Teddy again. "We took an Uber, smartass."

"Vince is by the pool out back." Teddy rubbed the back of his head. "Go straight through the main foyer to the hall on your left. That'll take you to him."

I clocked three werewolves, armed—two on the door and one just turning the corner toward the side of the house. While the driveway wasn't long—it only took us a few minutes to walk to the house—it was plenty of time for security to check us out. They didn't seem bothered to frisk us or anything, our reputations had likely preceded us, anyway. We weren't really the type of werewolves to carry, since our bodies *were* our weapons, so passing through the main door was anti-climactic.

The house was from another time, a century or more old and dripping with charm that I wouldn't have expected from a slick guy like Vincent was reported to be.

It was classy with its wrap-around porch, red brick and black shutters. I could see myself lounging on the two-person swing that hung just off the main entrance, sipping bourbon, enjoying the sunset with Charlie curled in next to me.

"This way," Lex said, pulling me out of my daydream. I pulsed my calm assessment of the property to Charlie, and she pulsed me back. *We're good.*

The inside was a stark contrast to the outside, which was a damn shame. Vincent had completely gutted the old-world charm of the place, obviously taking down walls and making the interior like a modern steel and glass monstrosity. It was a blasphemy. If I had a place like this, I'd preserve as much of the history as I could.

We exited to the back where a wide patio stretched in both directions, surrounding a huge crystal blue pool, complete with a waterfall.

"Welcome, welcome!" Vince was lying on a lounge chair in the sun, his oiled-up body glistening in a way that made me want to gag.

He had very tight, very minimal swim shorts on that left nothing to the imagination.

This was what he wore to a business meeting? Somehow not totally surprising but definitely not what I'd been prepared to see.

"Grab a seat," Vince waved to the shaded table on our right. "Tell Mani what you'd like to drink while I go get dressed."

I inwardly sighed. I didn't think I'd be able to take him seriously in his pool wear, but I badly wanted to snap a picture with my phone to show my guys so I could burn their retinas, too.

Mani came and went, drink orders taken then delivered. I opted for a mojito, while Lex had a beer.

Vince came back in a pair of white linen pants and a blue short-sleeved shirt that was unbuttoned to his waist.

He looked like a gigolo, about as smarmy as Charlie said he'd be.

"Johnny Duke, it's a pleasure," Vincent said as he offered his hand.

I took it, giving a firm shake. "Thank you for inviting me here."

"My nephew told me you have a proposition." Vincent nodded to Lex. "Something related to Kane's abandonment of the pack?"

You wish. "Yes, unfortunately, Kane felt he needed to leave."

"Which surprises me," Vincent said. "Considering he just laid down a small fortune for Charlotte Larsen."

"Well, you've heard, I'm sure, about her... abnormalities." It killed me to say those words, but I knew the end justified the means.

Vincent looked at me over the top of his sunglasses. "Indeed, I have. I believe Sal warned Kane about her particular deformity."

"About that..." I leaned forward, elbows on the table. "I'd like to see the contract. The original."

Vincent's eyes widened. "You have a copy. Surely Kane showed you."

"He did, yes, but my brother Levi, he detected a trace of witch text—"

"Whoa there, wait one minute!" Vince pushed his chair back. "It sounds like you're gearing up for an accusation."

"I'm just trying to find out what Kane kept from us." Another lie, another inner cringe. "We need to know what he signed us up for. Charlie... She's...a lot."

Vince slapped the table so it shook my drink and Lex grabbed his bottle in time before it tipped over. "Oh fuck yeah, I bet." He laughed again. "Now I understand. No refunds, boys. That was in the contract, I assure you."

"I'm not looking for a refund." I took a long haul from my drink, loving the tang that soaked my throat. "I'm looking for the loophole. Levi says there's more to the contract than what we have on ours. He suspects that Sal wrote something in there that might help us out." Vincent had no idea what Levi was capable of with his magic detecting ability. "Levi thinks Sal ultimately wants Charlie back. We're thinking we might be able to make that happen in a more mutually advantageous way."

Vincent leaned back in his chair to study me. "I've heard about your brother's ability to sense magic. He got all that from the top copy of your contract?"

That was confirmation that Levi had been right about a multi-layered document.

"He's got some special skills." I drained my drink. "So you think I can take a look? See what my useless older brother tied us to?"

"I might be able to help you." Vince rubbed his chin. "Sure, yeah, I could let you take a peek...for a favor."

I nodded and waved my hand. "Consider it done."

Vince smacked his knee as he stood. "You're my kind of man, Johnny, just like Lex said." He circled his finger around our drinks. "I'll get Mani to bring another round." He paused, his face turning serious. "No funny business, though. You so much as twitch like you're going to take the contract, and my dogs will rip you apart."

Three security guards stepped forward. His wolves were big, probably bad, but they were no match for Charlie.

"Vince, I just want to see what my brother agreed to so I can clean up his mess." I sighed, putting everything I had into the act.

Vince nodded. "The sins of our brothers rest heavy on our lives. I got you, Johnny."

He left, and I released the tension I was carrying. We were almost there.

When Vince came back, he was carrying a satchel that reeked of bad things. I didn't need Levi's ability to read magic to know that what was inside the bag was dangerous.

He tossed the leather case in front of me. "I've unlocked it so you can read the witch text." He raised his hands. "But don't shoot the messenger, eh? I had nothing to do with what's written there."

I didn't blame Kane for not detecting the magic text because even unlocked, it was barely a blip on my senses. Something felt off, yes, but not enough to make me want to investigate, just enough to make my hackles rise.

I held the contract, which was only one page, just like the one we had. This one, though, had iridescent script along the outside border of the paper. I turned the document to read all the way around.

First is the bite, three times three.
Next will ignite the power of she.
Then the beast will be locked on site.
Unable to step foot away, no matter her might.
Finally, the hunt will begin.

I reread the words three times, not sure I was understanding. This would be a piece of cake for Levi to decipher. *Witches and their nonsense riddles.*

"Can you translate this for me, Vince?" I turned the document his way.

Vince slipped into his chair, letting out a grunt that sounded like a laugh. "Those witches are something, right? Can't just say things plainly." He rubbed his hand over his head, smoothing his hair back before picking up his drink. "From what I've been told, the plan is for Charlie to complete some kind of predestined circle, get bitten by you three brothers, then turn into some kind of monster."

I kept my face neutral, not wanting to give anything away.

"Then she'll be locked down at the Duke compound, and Sal will bring more of his pet witches to take out your security fence." He leaned forward, a sick expression on his face. "And the hunt will begin." He raised his hand as he leaned back. "But hey, I'm just the messenger, and Sal is a sick fuck. Pays well, but yeah...a slimeball."

I leaned back, trying to keep it cool. I had a job to do, and this information was new but not totally surprising. "I assume he plans to take out the Duke clan while he's at it."

Vincent shrugs. "No need. When he kills her, your clan will transfer to him."

"Riiight." I steepled my fingers under my chin, channeling a bit of Kane. "I'd like to propose a new deal."

"Sal isn't known to negotiate, especially when he's winning." Vincent laughed as he pulled off his sunglasses. "But, for what it's worth, I'll let him know.

Now for my favor." He rubbed his hands together. "I want a night with Charlie." He grinned. "One night, no holds barred."

I wanted to rip his motherfucking throat out. "Probably not a good idea... She's wild—"

"Don't get me wrong. I'm not suicidal." Vince motioned to his throat. "I have a witch collar, and I want to see her on her knees. No biting, I promise."

"Awww, but all I want to do is bite, Vince-baby." Charlie came around the corner, blood dripping from her jowls, her claws red, in full beast mode.

Chapter Thirty-Two

Charlie

"I thought we'd agreed you'd wait for my signal." Johnny pushed his chair back—the clatter of metal hitting cement made my ears ring.

"I got bored." I swiveled on my heels then dove for the first of the three werewolves roaring toward me. They were fast. I'd give them that.

Levi caught another one mid-leap, and Johnny, now in his beast form, took out number three. Instead of a bloodbath, I sent the command through our link, *bite and secure*.

I was building an army, wasn't I?

I pinned down the one I'd caught, my knees on his chest as he fought to shift to his wolf. "Nah-uh, big guy, you're mine now." At the sound of Levi and Johnny doing their thing, I leaned in and took the bite.

It was over in a matter of seconds. My fur was sticky with blood, the humans at the gate and on the door had shot at me. I'd bitten them, too, but I doubted they'd make the transition to werewolf. The crystal-clear water in the pool made me want to dive in and get the worst of the gore off...but first...I turned to Vince where he still sat, under protest, in his chair. Lex had him pinned, his big black wolf twice the size of Vince in human form.

"Where were we?" I said as I left bloody footprints on the concrete, the *squish squish* of my beast feet squeezing it out of my fur damn near comical. "Oh yeah, we were talking about the renegotiation of a shit deal."

"You crazy bitch, you'll never get Sal to agree —"

I darted one monstrous arm out to grab Vince by the throat, cutting off his air, along with his voice.

"I don't need to get him to agree. You do." I pulled him close, his feet scraping along the ground as I hauled him to face level. "From now on, you work for me."

I flicked his jaw with my thumb, loosened my grip, then sank my fangs into the meaty flesh between his neck and shoulder.

Chapter Thirty-Three

You came to me from both sides of the ether world, parting the shadows with your bodies in human form. Two men, my men, you both have one purpose in mind, and I felt it like an electric shock along my skin.

I had quieted the noise from the pack I've been building, and all I could hear were your lusty needs. Johnny, your desire to chase me through the shadows made my legs twitch with pent-up energy. Levi, your thirst to trail kisses all over my flesh made goosebumps rise.

We, all three, basked in our triumph. We had conquered so much in such a short amount of time. Now we would celebrate.

Then we would do what needed to be done.

You took my body in your arms, naked flesh pressed to naked flesh. I felt your hard cock pressed against my stomach and another teasing along the seam of my ass. You tilted my head back then kissed me, your tongue probing, lips bruising mine. So penetrating. So demanding.

You kissed a line down the column of my throat, along my collarbone, around the outside curve of my breast. Your hands came around my sides, slid up my waist to cup my tits, fingers splayed around my aching nipples.

You sucked the hard buds, so I was arching against your lips, begging with my body for more.

You parted my legs with a hand on my thigh, trailing up to hold the vee of my pussy in your palm. Your heat was electrifying.

I was enveloped in pleasure as you parted my pussy lips then circled my clit.

I was lost to ecstasy as you devoured my mouth with punishing kisses.

I was floating in bliss as you both touched me with deft, unrelenting strokes.

* * * *

We came out of the shadow world, out from my mind, to find ourselves right where we'd started, entangled on my bed, our original purpose to sleep, now turned to pleasure.

Johnny was under me, his cock pushed against my ass, his hands holding my tits, with Levi hovering on top, sucking on my nipples, his fingers knuckle deep in my pussy, questing for my G-spot.

Exactly the kind of sandwich I was craving.

I arched into Levi at the same time I wedged my ass harder against Johnny's steel rod.

My hands were busy, one above my head, holding the back of Johnny's neck, fingers tangled in his long hair, the other gripping Levi's ass, urging him to go deeper with his fingers, press harder with his thumb.

Without needing direction, my men read my body language and knew what I needed. Levi slid his fingers free while Johnny released my lips so I could come up for air.

Levi ran a finger along the seam of my lips, coating me with my own juice as Johnny put his hands on my hips, gripping me tightly, digging his fingers into my flesh. I sucked Levi's fingers into my mouth then twirled my tongue over each of them, lapping up the taste of my arousal.

Levi's cock nudged against my pussy, positioned exactly where I wanted him to be.

Johnny's dick came at me from behind.

I had the craven thought that I could take them both at the same time, and before I could think twice, that was exactly what they did.

Two cocks, nudged at my hole, slowly, gingerly wedging themselves into me. I wiggled to accommodate them both, opening my legs wide while Levi sank down and Johnny arched up.

Levi kissed away the burn of my pussy spreading wider, drugging me with distraction while Johnny teased my nipples with one hand, his other still gripping my hip, branding me with his fingers.

Both cocks stretched me out, filled me up, made me want to writhe from both pain and pleasure.

The beast in me was wild with lust. I waited until they were fully seated, both cocks jammed into me, then I bucked, jolting the men into action.

Johnny pulled his cock almost all the way out while Levi pushed deeper in, the sensation sent shivers over my body and raised delicious goosebumps. After a moment, Levi pulled himself back to the tip, while Johnny pistoned into me, harder and faster than he had before.

They alternated their thrusts with perfect timing, never leaving me empty, rubbing along my G-spot,

Levi's fingers pressed against my clit, applying enough pressure to make stars dance across my vision.

There was no warning when my climax hit because there was no beginning or end to the pleasure I was feeling. It roared through me like a tsunami, washing over my body, pinging against every erogenous zone then bouncing back again.

Two cocks, pumping me up, hands everywhere on my body, a mouth on my lips and one nipping at my earlobe, bodies slick with sweat, rubbing and grinding all over me.

I didn't stand a chance.

My orgasm exploded again and again. A night sky full of fireworks flashed across my eyes. Spasms carried me over the edges, making me moan until my throat was hoarse. Levi followed first, groaning into my mouth as he filled me up with his cum. My pussy dripped as he pulled out to spew more of his load on my stomach while Johnny finished with hard, deep thrusts, spilling inside, a jet of heat that seared my pussy.

We collapsed into a tangled heap once again, finally satiated enough for sleep to pull us under just as we were.

Chapter Thirty-Four

Charlie

Groveling Andrew was not my favorite version of my stepbrother, but it was one I was resigned to endure now that he was Levi's minion.

He found me in the study with Johnny, escorted by a few members of the Duke pack, and had prostrated himself like he was praying to his new god...me. He held a stack of plastic covered sheets, offered up like a sacrifice.

"I got them, just as you asked. They're all here — the ones Sal had, anyway. I personally checked."

Gareth was in the infirmary with Levi. He'd taken a silver bullet to the gut and was being treated for the poison spread. I had cut off his pain with a simple thought almost immediately, an act of mercy I could give to those bitten by me. One I knew that he knew, I could take back at any time. His sappy gratitude had been almost nauseating. I'd cut the volume of that off, too.

Ruby had been moved to a comfortable suite on the third floor. Her watchmen, Lex, Ari and Rue were taking turns keeping an eye on her. The sedation we'd been administering, along with my pulses of calm sent through our threaded link, had been keeping her stable and mostly out of it, but the full moon was a day away, and the true effect of my bite was yet to be seen.

For now, we needed to figure out the part of the story that my stepbrother knew and we didn't.

Johnny took the scrolls then placed them on the long table where the ones we had lay.

"You're dismissed, Andrew, but stay close. We might need you again," Levi said as he walked in the room. He had the man by the balls, using his bite connection to Andrew in a more dominating way than was usual — a necessary evil for the time being, until we decided what we wanted Andrew's role to be in the pack.

"Yes, of course. I'll be in the kitchen, if that's okay? I haven't eaten since —"

"Just go, Andrew. You don't need to ask permission to feed yourself, for fuck's sake," Levi snapped, a tired whip to his voice.

Andrew bowed as he walked out of the room, and I rolled my eyes at Johnny. "What the fuck did Levi do to him?"

"Not enough I'm sure," Johnny laughed. He was bent over the table, studying the depictions on the scrolls. "I think I have them in order now."

I followed the path of his finger as he pointed along the story before us.

"Three bite marks here," I noted.

Johnny shifted the next picture closer. "Is that what you'll look like after you have Kane's bite?" The picture showed a beastly female glowing like she was radioactive.

"Fuck, I hope not." I squinted. "Is she flying?"

"Floating? She's definitely not touching the ground." Levi squeezed in between us, taking the scroll from Johnny.

"That's got to be figurative." I hoped.

"Maybe you'll be floating on a high because you're bonded with the Duke brothers," Johnny teased, a swat to my ass behind Levi's back made me yelp.

Levi cocked an eyebrow but didn't peel his eyes from the picture in his hand.

"Look though...here." Johnny pointed to the next picture. "If that isn't Sal..."

A black wolf was on the hunt, chasing the beast. It gave me a chill. The uncanny similarity to my stepbrother put a knot in my stomach.

"Why is she running if she's all powerful?" Levi frowned as he took the next scroll from Johnny.

"He's got something in his teeth." I pointed at what looked like a knife with gems. It shone from the black wolf's mouth like it was reflecting moonlight. "Maybe it's a talisman or something." Familiarity hit like a smack upside the head. "Dad had something like this in one of the display cases in his den." I remembered always wanting to touch it, but my father wouldn't let me get near it. "Fuck, I'd forgotten about it."

"All right, so it's safe to say that Sal has figured out a way to put these pieces together — and that that blade might be a means of hurting you." Levi dropped the scroll, hunting for the next one.

"I can't see how... It's just a knife." I didn't want to believe the parts of this story that were evolving into something fantastical. A knife meant to kill me? In my father's possession? No, he'd never be so careless. "Even if it was silver...it wouldn't—"

"It's a ceremonial blade, and it's kind of what I expected to see," Levi said as he moved around me to the other side of the table. "Our mother said there'd be tools."

He picked up the next scroll to examine it.

"This shows two paths diverging." Levi traced the lines until they went off the sheets.

The beast was on one path. The wolf was about to cut her off.

"Two possible outcomes?" Johnny entwined his fingers with mine, pulling me into his side.

"Looks that way." Levi, so focused on the scroll that he didn't seem to notice Levi's move into my space. He picked up the last scroll we had. It showed the black wolf standing on the dead body of the beast. "Triumphant."

"But there's another outcome if there's another path," I said, unwilling to accept the version of events that the last picture laid out. "This says twelve of fifteen. There are three pictures missing."

"Looks that way," Levi finally looked up, noted how close Johnny and I were then scowled. "We need to find the other scrolls."

"Which are where?" Somewhere impossible to get to, I was sure.

"Italy. In the vaults of the scholars," Levi said. "I think that's where we'll find Kane, too. If I were him, I'd have gone there. He'll want to know how the story ends."

"How would he know that there are two paths?" I recalled Kane's final words to me. How he'd said he wanted to get the truth. "He hasn't seen these scrolls."

"He probably has, though," Johnny said, surprising us both. "He once told me that Dominic invited him to his house for dinner once—when we were all young, and Kane had just formed the pack."

Of course! Dad had always felt Kane was on his way to success. He would have offered support, encouragement. "My father could have shown him these scrolls."

"I think he did...because he told Kane that in a few years, the Duke brothers would be an integral part of the Larsen conglomerate." Levi shuffled the scrolls together, gently placing them in a neat pile. "At the time, Kane thought he meant some kind of business deal, but now I'm realizing that he meant something bigger. He advised Kane to start hunting down the rest of the scrolls."

"My dad knew. He knew what was going to happen. All of it." I stumbled back a step. "That means Kane knew, too. He knew about the three bites."

"Kane didn't know. He would have told me, if he had figured it out. He just said that your dad showed him a bunch of ancient artifacts...papers, a blade. Your dad only let him take a quick look, not enough time to study and understand them," Levi said. "He mentioned it to me like your dad was quirky—not like, this is tied to our family's prophecy."

"The stories your father told you..." Johnny turned me toward him. "He was trying to tell you—"

"Fairy tales..."

"About your destiny," Johnny finished.

"So this is all inevitable? No avoiding it?" I didn't know why, after everything that had happened so far, I was still in denial.

"Looks that way." Levi pointed to the scroll. "But there's an alternative ending, and somewhere deep down in his thick skull, Kane knows it. He'll want to figure how it ends so he can make sure it works for us."

"How it *could* end," Johnny said.

"How it *will* end," I said, motioning for Levi to come to me. "Let's go get Kane. He and I are due for a heart-to-heart."

It was time for me to get my man and put our own twist on how this story would end.

Want to see more from this author?
Here's a taster for you to enjoy!

Hell Hath No Fury: Wrath
Angela Addams

Coming Summer 2024

Excerpt

Charlie

For a born werewolf, the full moon would bring nature into balance. A night filled with fun, games and satiation of all senses.

For a newly bitten werewolf, that very same bloom in the night sky would bring chaos, pain and often, especially for females, death.

I stared out through the floor-to-ceiling windows in the hallway just next to the guest suite and let the iridescent glow bathe me, soothe me, wash me of my sins.

You wish, my beastly darker half grunted, not so much in words as in scalding attitude.

Cynical bitch.

By the sounds coming from inside the room next to me, I knew that the worst of my sins was, in fact, wishing me dead this very moment.

I hoped Ruby would forgive me at some point so she could see that happen—my death, that was—when we were both into our two-hundreds and speckled gray old gals. We could die together, on the same day even, so we'd never have to feel the loss of one another's presence.

That was how I'd always envisioned best friends, found sisters, would live and die.

Never having had one in my life, I obviously got some things wrong.

For one, she was human...or had been less than three days ago, incompatible with my very — death to anyone human who knew — secret werewolf existence.

Two, before now, she had no idea that werewolves existed, because, well, as mentioned, it was immediate death to humans who knew that monsters of lore were, in fact, real.

Three, she was about to become one herself, which would likely kill her.

So yeah, best friends forever — but only if she survived the night. After that, I'd be grateful if she didn't hate me for more than a handful of decades.

With my bite, a powerful, werebeast alpha's bite, my best friend, my *now* pack-mate Ruby's transformation could go either way. I didn't know enough about how my werebeast bite would take to a female human. As far as I knew, it had only happened thousands of years ago when female warriors built armies of werebeasts like her, but those days had died long before I'd been born — so long ago, in fact, that their existence had been wiped from our shared history by the patriarchal alphas who ruled the clans today.

There was no current proof that what I'd done to Ruby in an effort to save her life would work out in a positive way. My beastly instincts said differently, maddeningly confident that this, too, would pass, that Ruby would rise and be stronger than she'd ever been as a human, a worthy and formidable soldier in my ever-growing army.

I could only hope for the best and put what little faith I had that my ancient beastly awareness knew what we were doing.

Ruby would only growl through gritted teeth whenever I entered her room, a lash of fury that stung me through the bond my bite had created. She had made it very clear that I'd ruined her life.

She wasn't wrong.

Which was why I hadn't been up to visit all day. Like a coward, I'd been preoccupying myself with other things.

I sighed deeply then pulled myself away from the call of the night. Johnny and Levi, my devoted mates, were blowing off steam in the sprawling forest outside the mansion, expecting me to join them for a full moon fuc —

The door beside me opened. Lex, Ruby's ever-present guard wolf, stepped outside of the room, pulling my attention out of my completely inappropriate lusty thoughts. I knew my cheeks were ruddy as I turned to greet him.

"How is she?" It was a silly question, considering I could open the threads connecting me to Ruby and feel her mood for myself, but I asked anyway, because I wasn't in the right frame of mind to feel the crushing disappointment and loathing Ruby had for me.

Like I said…coward.

Lex gave me a look that made things as clear as the night sky.

Things are not *good.*

"She's still fighting the shift" — Lex ran his hand over the back of his neck, making it look like he was the one going through a painful transition as he gritted his teeth around his next word — "somehow."

We both knew that Ruby fighting the shift would only lead to bad things.

More pain.

Mental anguish.

Delayed transformation would mean, like tectonic plates shifting, the pressure would build up inside Ruby and the shift would come suddenly, against her will and with devastating consequences.

Broken bones.

Lots of blood.

Death.

Or worse, for Ruby and for all of us, she could turn feral in the most horrific, wild, uncontrollable ways. There was no coming back from that kind of break from reality. She'd give in to every base instinct and would ultimately put the secret world we'd lived in for centuries at risk of exposure. It was a death sentence to her, no matter what.

"Stubborn." Was an understatement when it came to what Ruby was doing. "How does she even have the strength left?" It was a marvel, a true example of what a remarkable human Ruby was, that she was even conscious right now. The fact that she'd spent the last twelve hours punishing herself, working against the change as the full moon crested the clear night sky.

"I think she's running on pure hate right now." Lex laughed as he said that, like his words weren't a slap to my face. "She tried to bite Ari when he suggested she was wasting her time fighting the inevitable, that she should just accept her blessing." Lex rolled his eyes. "Not what she wanted to hear...considering..."

"What idiot told her she wouldn't be able to have kids now, anyway?" I snapped then regretted it immediately. "Sorry." I closed my eyes as Ruby groaned in the next room. "It's not your fault, any of you. *I* did this to her."

"Hey," Lex said as he took me off guard and laid his hands on my shoulders, a gesture that was a huge no-no for any subordinate to an alpha but one that I didn't mind. His lopsided smile was enough to hijack any antiquated werewolf protocols.

Besides, I wasn't the usual kind of alpha.

And I wasn't Lex's alpha. Not yet anyway.

"You saved her life." His smile faded enough to tell me that he believed his own words. "Without your bite, she'd be dead right now. It *is* a blessing."

"She doesn't see it that way." I'd taken the one thing away from Ruby that she's desired more than anything else, a chance to have her own children one day.

Never mind that it hadn't been me who had bitten her the first time. That lovely gift had been from her ex, a man who went after what he thought was a coyote with a pipe only to find out that werewolves didn't back down from humans...*ever.*

Jared's fang scratch to Ruby's thumb, a wound that might have gone unnoticed if I hadn't been paying attention to her discomfort, would have killed her within a day. He'd been too newly formed, too weak to successfully bite another human, but he'd been crazed, confused and had attacked her without realizing what he was doing was irreversible. Ruby wouldn't have made it to the full moon, three days after her initial bite.

According to her, Ruby would have taken death over what was happening to her now. To her, oblivion was a safer choice than becoming one of us. Again, not something I blamed her for. There'd been times in my life that I'd wished I'd never been born a werewolf.

"No one told her, by the way," Lex said, his voice void of all humor, "about the babies."

I should have told her. I should have been the one to explain everything to her. I'd bitten her, stabilized her, she'd woken up and had been coherent. I could have told her.

"Levi explained what would happen to her body," Lex continued.

I held my hand up for him to stop. I knew the rest.

She'd figured it out.

Of course, she had. Ruby was whip smart and cut through the crap better than anyone I'd ever known.

Levi would have told her that her organs were going to die, some she'd expel, which was why transformation was so painful and deadly. Some would shift into something else, organs more powerful and able to handle the demands of a werewolf. Systems would no longer function the way they used to. They'd improve efficiently and handle hormones and chemicals differently. He would have told her that she would become immune to most diseases, that she wouldn't get viruses, that she wouldn't grow cells that were foreign to her body, no cancer…no warts, no *other* things.

She would have known immediately what that meant.

No possibilities of having babies of her own.

"The guys and I were talking," Lex said, plowing through my silence. "We think you need to do your mind meld thing. Make the transition happen."

"Against her wishes." I'd already bitten her without consent. Like Lex said, I'd done it to save her life. I'd gone on instinct and had allowed my beast side to take control, mark Ruby, end her suffering by delivering her to the prison she now found herself in.

A newly turned werewolf. A rare female in a male-dominated world...bitten and barren.

Lex was right, though. No matter how hard Ruby fought, the change would come, with or without her sanity intact. I had the ability to ease her pain and lower her guard enough to let the shift happen.

I closed my eyes, let my shoulders drop, sucked in a deep breath then nodded. I'd already ruined her life beyond repair. Might as well go for a homerun and force her to survive what Jared...what *I*, had done to her.

Lex opened the door to the sounds of agony. Ruby was whimpering, begging without words for someone to put her out of her misery. It sounded like a wounded animal trapped in claws of steel.

I couldn't see her yet, standing just outside her room, but I could feel her despair. It was more than pain. It was heartbreak and grief. She'd lost her life and everything she'd loved. There was no going back to family, to friends. I deserved to know the depths of her anguish.

I shook off my fear, straightened my spine, held my head high like an alpha should, then swept into the room, pulsing calm vibes down the thread that tied Ruby to me and opened myself up to the full force of her pain. It took everything in me to stay on my feet, to endure the anger, sorrow and physical agony of her fight.

As soon as she came into view, I froze, swaying on my feet. Ruby, while still mostly human, looked like a wild thing on all fours, covered in sweat, hair sprouting in ways that looked unnatural and incomplete. Her eyes, now locked on mine, were blazing with werewolf intensity.

Normally warm brown, they shone bronze with a glint that promised reckoning. I didn't need an open thread between us to feel the depth of her fury.

"You!" she growled, spit flying from her lips. "*You* did this to me!" Her words were garbled as fangs got in the way of her tongue.

"Ruby—"

She lurched toward me, swiping her hand like she had claws. Before she could get within reach, she screamed, her neck distorting as it lengthened, her spine popping so loud that we all felt it. A sympathetic groan ran through the room. She fell in a heap, sobbing.

"Make it stop," she begged, clawing at her torso. The fabric of her hospital gown torn where her budding claws had raked. She rolled onto her back, arching through the pain as it racked her.

I didn't have to look at the guys to know what they thought.

I moved to Ruby cautiously, opening the thread that connected us wider so I could ease my essence toward her, giving her peace, sedation for her brain.

She stopped writhing and gouging at her body. Her arms fell limp across her stomach.

"Ruby, it's just going to happen, okay?" I got within her reach, but she didn't lash out again, instead, her eyes dull, she stared, unblinking at the ceiling.

"Let me help you." I lowered myself next to her slowly, like I was working with a wild animal, a wolf in pain. Not that I was afraid she'd hurt me... Whatever she decided to do to my flesh, I deserved it.

I needed some sign of consent.

I wanted to give her a lot of time to stop me. To say no.

I ran my fingers through her hair, brushing what was left of her bangs from her distorted forehead. "Please, Rubes, let me help you through this."

She groaned as another ripple ran through her body, tension making her muscles pop and her veins darken. A drawn-out minute passed before she curled in on herself as best as she could, rolling to the side, tears running down her cheeks where fur was trying to push out of her pores.

I slipped my other hand under her head and eased her weight onto my lap. She let me hold her like that, and it gave me some comfort. I sent soothing pulses through our link, giving her instant relief so that her gritted teeth were the only lingering sign that another spasm was rocking down her spine.

"I'm sorry, Ruby," I croaked, tears burning the backs of my eyes. "I didn't mean for this to happen."

She shifted her gaze to the side, locking with mine, her shuddering subsiding to small shivers. I pulsed more of my essence, my will, into her. *Be calm, my friend. Let the fight go.*

Her body went limp, but she managed to turn her head so she was staring full on at me.

"I will never forgive you for this, Charlie." She licked her lips, snagging her tongue on her fangs as she did, blood spurting from a new wound, coating her teeth. "*Never.*"

My heart, already in shreds, fell apart for good. "I know, Rubes," I whispered. "I wish it were different."

"I wish I'd never met you," she breathed.

With a body shaking exhale, she transformed, the last of her physical humanity shifting away as she became the wolf she was meant to be—brown fur, so soft to the touch that it set her apart from the males I knew, rippling muscles down her flank, long legs, elegant paws with tuffs of tawny fur between her toes. Her muzzle was sleek, marked by freckles, just like she had as a human, her lashes thick and her whiskers black. She was beautiful...stunning in only the way a female werewolf could be.

My heart swelled and pride cascaded along our bond. She'd done it, come through unscathed.

In one delusional moment, I thought that the physical transformation might have jolted her back to her old self. I wished that was the case, anyway. A future without Ruby's friendship was devastating.

By the way she pushed apart from me — standing on all fours, inches from my face, muzzle down and scrunched, lips up, fangs gleaming and bronze eyes holding the same knowing, the same conviction as before her shift — I knew...

As far as Ruby was concerned, I was her enemy.

About the Author

Angela Addams is an author of many naughty things. She believes that the written word is an amazing tool for crafting the most erotic of scenarios and likes telling stories about normal people getting down and dirty and falling in love. Enthralled by the paranormal at an early age, Angela also spends a lot of her time thinking up new story ideas that involve supernatural creatures in everyday situations.

She is an avid tattoo collector, a total book hoarder, and loves anything covered in chocolate…except for bugs.

She lives in Ontario, Canada in an old, creaky house, with her husband, children and four moody cats.

Angela loves to hear from readers. You can find her contact information, website details and author profile page at https://www.totallybound.com

Home of Erotic Romance

Sign up for our newsletter and find out about all our
romance book releases, eBook sales and promotions,
sneak peeks and FREE romance books!